The Club of Clubs

The Club of Clubs

By

Charles Martinez

iUniverse, Inc.
Bloomington

The Club of Clubs

iUniverse books may be ordered through booksellers or by contacting:

iUniverse
1663 Liberty Drive
Bloomington, IN 47403
www.iuniverse.com
1-800-Authors (1-800-288-4677)

ISBN: 978-1-4620-2460-5 (sc)
ISBN: 978-1-4620-2461-2 (e)

Printed in the United States of America

iUniverse rev. date: 10/31/2011

For my father, whose stories of old El Paso
planted the seeds for this one.

1

The words of an old cop came into my thoughts as I walked through the deserted police station on my way home. *The world will be rid of crime when it is rid of hunger.* It seemed to me that he had spoken the words softly and to no one in particular, and I wondered now in the stillness of the station if maybe he had meant other kinds of hunger and not simply the one in a person's stomach. There were quite a few, really.

My hand was on the lever of the door when the telephone began to ring at the front desk. I waited. On the third loud ring Sergeant Kane came quickly out of the restroom off to one side. I heard him speak into the mouthpiece. "Yes, yes, he is just now walking out the door." He turned to me and called out, "Hey, Vince, hold on." Kane held the telephone slightly away from his ear, as though whoever was on the other end was speaking loudly. He listened for a moment and then he put the telephone back on the cradle. I didn't hear him say goodbye.

"The Chief." Kane said. "He's called Evan back from vacation. The Chief wants you to meet Evan at Ninth and Campbell right away." Just then, a man with blood all over his jacket and a wild-eyed young woman came walking in the door. They were handcuffed together and taking turns cursing each other. Behind them came an officer whose name I could not recall and behind him came a blast of cold air. Kane motioned the three of them to a bench along the wall.

As I walked back toward the high desk, Kane took his handkerchief out of his pocket and began drying his hands. He kept his eyes down, looking at his hands, as he spoke to me. "Something tells me we might be back to the crap of three years ago." Kane grimaced. "Today is the fifth, Vince, November the fifth." He spoke the word *fifth* in a strange manner.

"Three years ago?" I moved closer to the desk. "Club?"

Kane looked at me. His eyes said yes.

I walked back around behind the desk and poured a cup or so of coffee from the urn into my thermos. Kane began moving stacks of paper this way and that, trying to put things in order. I thought of Penny waiting for me at home. I thought of the wine and the warmth of the firelight.

"Kane," I said, "can you call Penny and tell her I'll be late?"

"What?"

"Call Penny for me, tell her I'll be— "

"Yeah, sure, Vince. Get going." I buttoned up my coat and got going.

As I turned on Stanton Street and headed south, a windblown sheet of newspaper landed on my windshield. I braked, and in that moment I felt the altogether odd sensation of déjà vu. In a flash, I was struck by the certainty that every single detail of tonight— Kane's words, the look on the young woman's face, the way my hand shook when I inserted the key into the ignition—all of those things had happened exactly that same way before. I was wondering what all that could mean when I arrived at the corner of Ninth and Campbell. A curved lamp, swaying in the wind, hung above the entrance to a grocery store. The lamp cast its dim light on a rusty metal sign, which read *"La Campana."* I duly noted the date, time, and location.

In addition to Evan's unmarked silver and navy-blue Buick, there were three police cars parked in front of the store. I could hear the siren of another car on the way. There was a crowd of twenty-five to thirty people among which there were several reporters including Octavio Ochoa, the reporter for one of the Juarez newspapers, who had written extensively about the previous homicides and who had named them the "Club of Clubs Murders." His articles had been picked up by newspapers all over the Southwest. The articles made Mr. Ochoa famous.

Three years prior, during the fall of 1950, and during which time I had been a rookie policeman, a strange and sensational series of homicides had placed the city in a stranglehold of terror. There was no other description for it. The murders had been committed in the Southside of the city of El Paso on the fifth day of the months of October, November, and December. The victims, elderly Mexican men who had been in the process of becoming United States citizens, had been shot to death at night in the kitchens of their homes. The killer had left a playing card at the scene of each crime. The killer, or killers, since we had not been able to rule out any possibility, had left the four of clubs at the scene in October, the three of clubs in November, and the two of clubs in December. The fingerprints on the cards had been made by the same person but no match for those prints had been found in either the El Paso or Juarez, Mexico police department files. The crimes remained unsolved but not forgotten. Fear and failure have a way of hanging around.

In the glow of my headlights I could see a bottle being passed around. A civilian was pulling a kerosene heater on metal wheels toward the crowd. An officer was roping off the area between the crowd and the store. I took one last sip of coffee from my thermos, slipped on my gloves, and stepped out of the car into a swirling wind.

As soon as Evan came out of his car, the reporters' cameras began to flash. He was impeccably dressed as always, a study in tan and brown. Evan and I approached the store together where Officer Teo Steele was standing at the door. Teo began speaking loudly, above the wind. "I'm getting too old to go through this shit again, Evan. The hell with this crap. I've got twenty-five years. I'll retire before..." He paused for a moment, cursed long and loud, and then started over. "Victim's name is Maximo Solares. Owner of the store. Sixty, sixty-five maybe. Shot in the chest. No robbery. The card is on the counter. Ace of damn clubs. Time of death is 10:00 p.m., according to the eyewitness. Young boy, nine years old. Tee is back there with him."

Evan took a few steps to the side to get a better angle at the inside of the brightly lit store. He stood there for a few moments and then came back, sparks flying from his lighter as he tried to light a cigarette. The wind carried the sound of a church bell clanging from across the river.

"You sure about the victim's name?" Evan asked Steele, who had cupped his hands and was blowing into them.

"That's what the license in there says, Evan."

Evan lit his cigarette. "How about that crowd? Has anyone questioned them?"

I could not hear Steele's response. Evan gestured with his head and Steele moved away toward the crowd. He picked out one of the men standing there and ordered him to approach. Evan opened the back door to his car and motioned for me to get in. He got in after me and closed the door, removing his hat as he did so. The flashing lights of the police car behind us gave his salt and pepper hair a slightly bluish tint.

Evan did not speak right away. He smoked his cigarette and looked straight ahead. I waited. He turned toward the window, away from me, and said something under his breath. Finally, he looked at me and spoke. "The Chief called me on this." Evan took a drag from his cigarette, exhaling very slowly. After a few moments, he spoke again. "You were aware that Tommy returned to the force?"

I was. Tommy Torres had been Evan's partner for twelve years but shortly after the last Club homicide he had left the force to establish his own private detective agency. Six months after that I was promoted to detective. I had heard through the grapevine that Torres' venture into the private eye business had not gone well. He had asked for his job back and been reinstated as a detective with no loss to seniority but had not been reassigned as Evan's partner.

Evan extinguished his cigarette in the pullout ashtray of the backside of the front seat. "The Chief said that Tommy is to join us in this investigation, since he was my partner on the other three."

I looked out to the street through the windshield. A dust devil of twigs and leaves moved in a straight line along the curb away from us. I had never seen a dust devil in the fall or winter, only in the summer. I wondered at the strangeness of it. I watched as it doubled in size, jumped the curb, and obliterated itself against the trunk of a bare cottonwood tree.

I cleared my throat. I'd been expecting this ever since Torres' return but I was disappointed that it should happen now. "You are saying that I am being assigned to another partner?"

A gust of wind shook the car. Evan said something I did not catch, then "...no, Tommy will be the third man." I was relieved at

Evan's words but there was a look in his eyes I had not seen before. It was different somehow, and one I couldn't read.

I thought about the atmosphere around the police department during the time of the other three murders. The newspapers had had quite a time with us. What emerged much too clearly, as far as we were concerned, was a dismal picture of the police force. It seemed that every day the newspapers asked the same question: What exactly was the El Paso police department doing to apprehend the serial killer of elderly Mexicans? Still, in spite of everything, we had followed up on dozens upon dozens of leads that regretfully always led to dead ends. For most of us the frustration of that time still hung around our necks.

Chief Hansen himself, on the day I was hired, told me that the great difficulty with law enforcement in South El Paso was that in addition to the numerous pachuco gangs, who had their own ideas about territory and revenge, there were also factions within this section of the city where the Mexican Revolution had not ended in 1920. Not by a long shot. It had merely moved across the border. There were men in that section of the city with a great passion for avenging old betrayals and injustices. Chief Hansen told me one of the gangs had begun to call itself "The Dead Avengers." I had never heard that name. It was like a joke. A deadly joke, he added.

He also told me something I already knew. There were killers available for hire from across the river. Cheap. An individual could swim or wade across the river, do the deed, go back, and disappear forever since you could hire someone else to do him whenever he got back to the other side. I gathered from the Chief's words that our only edge was that we had a number of undercover people and informants on both sides of the river and the full cooperation, as a rule, of the Juarez police.

As these thoughts were crossing my mind, a man moved away from the crowd. Swaying and stumbling, wine bottle in hand, the man stepped over the low rope as Evan rolled down his window. The drunk yelled, *"Orale maestro, un tragito pues."* Then, leaning into the open window, the man said in a clear, sober voice: "Woman dressed in black running north on Campbell, ten o'clock."

"Check." Evan said, as the man staggered back toward the crowd.

"Are you familiar with the layout here, Vinny?" Evan asked.

This section of the Second Ward had been my beat before I became a detective. All the tenements in this area were basically the same. They were very old, very cramped, block-long structures in the shape of brackets with an alley running between them. They were all three-room units except for the corners, which were five or six rooms each and usually contained a business such as a grocery store or restaurant or some kind of shop. Directly behind the tenements would be a long row of outhouses. In this case the opening in the back would be wider still since a canal ran there also. On either side of the canal ran an eight-foot high wire fence.

On a night very much like this one I had chased a suspect behind this tenement some three years before. They called him "Little Red." I never knew his real name. He had jumped that fence. With one high leap, turning his body as he jumped, he was able to grab the top of the fence with his right hand and hook his elbow over it and then he had fired two shots at me. I fell to the ground and fired back. He dropped his rifle, a sawed-off .22, and swung up and over the fence and landed on his feet at the edge of the canal. He then dove headfirst into the water and disappeared. Thinking that he would go downstream and then surface, I had run in that direction. He did not come up so I ran upstream. How he had been able to get away I could never figure out but I never saw him again.

"Yes, I am familiar." I answered.

"Okay. Go in through the back." Evan said. "Miss nothing, assume nothing. Interview the boy."

I opened the door as Evan stepped out of the car on his side. "Remember, Vinny," he called out, "the obvious is not always correct."

"Right." I said, as I moved away.

I walked along the sidewalk on the Campbell Street side of the store. It was very cold. As I was walking by the long window of the store, the crime scene photographer inside moved to his left and squatted down slightly. I saw the victim. His face was large and round and it rested on the counter. His eyes were open, looking straight at me. At that moment the light bulb flashed its brilliant white, burning a stark and shadowless picture of death into my brain.

I reached the opening to the back of the tenement and waited a minute or so to allow my vision to return to normal. There was a narrow path between some oleander bushes and the canal fence. The windblown ripples on the canal reflected a fractured moon. I ran my flashlight along the path and forced the thought of "Little Red" out of my mind.

The back of the tenement was neat and windswept. I could see the long row of outhouses in the moonlight. Washtubs of various sizes hung on hooks along the tenement walls. I retraced my steps along the path and double-checked for anything I might have missed. I walked back to the first door down from the corner and knocked. My pulse quickened. I would miss nothing.

2

Officer Sam Tee opened the door and let me in to the kitchen, which was lighted by a bright light bulb hanging from the ceiling. The linoleum floor, an arabesque design of brown and blue, looked and smelled new. There were two curtained doorways, one led toward the store area and the other toward what would be a bedroom. There was a small gas stove against the outside wall on which there was a pot of coffee just beginning to percolate. Next to the stove was a sink with a round mirror above it. On the wall that abutted the next unit there was a refrigerator, on top of which there was a framed picture. Next to the refrigerator was a cupboard.

In the middle of the small kitchen there was a square wooden table with a clean white tablecloth, starched and pressed. There were three chairs, two wooden ones and a metal one with shiny, curved chrome legs. In one corner there was an ashtray on a stand.

I directed my attention to the photograph on the refrigerator as Sam sat down and turned a page on his newspaper. In the picture there were three men seated at a table. The man in the middle was Pancho Villa. The location of the photograph appeared to be the ice cream parlor on the corner of Stanton and Paisano. There was a small empty bowl in front of each man. Villa appeared to be in his late twenties, virile and muscular. He was well dressed and well groomed. His bloused boots were highly polished, his legs together. His hands were crossed, one atop the other. He looked almost prim. The two men sitting with him looked slightly older. One was lean, the other not so. They were serious looking men, intimidating. Men not to be trifled with.

Incidental to, and not with the same sharp clarity of the men, were two women sitting at the counter. They were facing each other. They resembled each other, both were very pretty. One was smiling faintly and reminded me of someone but I could not remember who. I estimated the picture to be perhaps forty years old, taken at some time during the Mexican Revolution.

As I studied the picture in its entirety the light, shadow, and subjects I was struck by its professionalism. I concluded that it had been expertly composed. And then, in the far background, almost blending into the shadows until I saw him, was a tall thin man. I could not tell if he was young or old. The janitor perhaps, for he was leaning on a broom. His elbows stuck out like wings. Yes, I thought, there could be no other reason for his presence in the picture. From the shadows he patiently surveyed the living. He represented Death.

I motioned Sam into the room leading to the store. The room was apparently a storage area but there was a narrow bed along one wall. The room smelled of soap. There were shelves, two high, around three walls on which there were canned goods and other sundries neatly stacked. The wall without shelves had a closet and the bed. The room was adjacent to the store area and another room. The curtain to that room was half open through which I could see a stuffed chair and a sofa with a sarape over it. There were papers scattered about the floor. Toward the store area, I heard the sound of movement and low conversation. I heard Evan direct the photographer to take a picture from behind the body. The room lit up with the reflection of the flash. Outside, the wind howled.

I heard something crash. Sam said, "Tubs flying, man." In a low voice I asked Sam if he had questioned the boy.

"Yes, he is a sharp little guy. You'll see…talks like a grown up. Says he was staying with a friend over on Florence for the weekend. Says he was supposed to come back here in the morning in time for school but came back tonight instead. Remembered he had homework."

"What did he see?"

"Said he was sitting on the sofa reading when he heard the bell over the door. He looked up through a crack in the curtain and saw a tall woman walk in. She was dressed in black with a black veil over her face. She pulled a pistol from her coat and pulled the trigger. Pistol misfired. Woman cursed. Victim began to rise from his chair when she fired again. This time the boy heard the explosion and hit the floor."

"How is the boy related to the victim?"

"Calls him uncle, but the boy's sister, who is also back there, says they are distant cousins."

"Sister?"

"Yes. One of the translators down at the courts. I'm sure you know her. Rosalinda. Can't remember her last name."

"What?" I said, louder than I intended.

"Yeah, you know, Rosalinda. Good looking girl, works down…"

I was no longer listening to Sam. I was thinking about Rosalinda Lucero. Yes, I knew her. I walked back across the kitchen toward the curtained doorway of the bedroom. I stopped and took a deep breath and then another, and then I entered.

3

The bedroom was candlelit. There was no bulb in the light fixture hanging from the ceiling. Three candles burned in rose-colored glass jars on a small table in front of a small religious statue. There was a mirror propped up on a table and against the wall. A young boy sat on the bed to my left. A voice said, "Oh, it's you." Then some unclear words. Then, "We were expecting Detective Morrow." In the shadows beside the bed sat Rosalinda. She was wearing a blue terry cloth robe. At that moment, the young boy rose quickly from the bed and walked toward me, hand extended.

"Benito Lucero, *a sus ordenes*." I bent down and shook his hand. "Hello, young man. I am Detective Quiñones. Are you all right?"

"Physically all right" he said. "But as you can see…" He did not finish as he waved his hand in the direction of the store. I said, "Yes, I understand. I'm sorry. That was your uncle?"

"Thank you, sir. We called him *tio*. But Rose says we were distant cousins."

I turned to Rosalinda. "Were you here when it happened, Miss Lucero?"

"No, I was not, Mr.… pardon me, Detective Quiñones." Her voice was as hard as I expected. She stressed the word *detective*, and I knew why. Catching the tone of his sister's voice the boy stepped back a pace and said, "Sir, may I see your badge?" From the inside chest pocket of my overcoat, I produced my badge in its black leather case and opened it. The boy took it from my hand and walked over to study it by the light of the candles. I wanted to smile at his seriousness but resisted.

The wind was blowing in gusts. The sound of the wind rose and fell like a moan. A branch scratched at the window. Benito came back and handed my badge back to me. I looked at Rosalinda and asked her where she had been at the time.

"At church."

"Yes, she was at church," said Benito, "she always goes to church on Sunday nights."

"And you arrived here when?" I asked her.

She answered without looking at me. "A little after ten."

I turned my attention to the boy. I asked him to tell me everything he knew.

"Well, my friend Mario and his older brother walked me back here at nine. I swept the store and restocked a few things. Then, I sat on the sofa and started my homework. It was very windy and cold. No one came in. Tio was sitting at the counter reading the newspaper. I heard the bell above the door. The curtain was open a little. A woman dressed in black with a black hat and a black veil over her face walked in. Tio said *'buenas'* and she said *'buenas'.*" Benito paused and said, "It's strange."

"What is strange?" I asked.

"Well, Tio Maximo was a man but he had kind of a woman's voice, and that woman, well, it looked like a woman, but she spoke in a man's voice."

From the corner of my eye I could see Rosalinda fidget. "Perhaps," she said, "it was a woman with a deep voice." *Like yours,* I thought.

Benito looked at her and said, "Maybe so."

"Benny," I said, "Do you mind if I call you Benny?"

"No sir. That's what they call me at school."

"Okay, Benny. Please continue."

"I think she asked for a pack of cigarettes and tio said something like 'what kind' and she said this kind and from inside her coat pocket she pulled out a pistol, raised it and fired. But there was a loud click and the gun didn't go off. Tio kept a pistol hidden underneath the counter but he didn't, or, I didn't see him reach for it. And then the woman said, '*chingada madre*' and fired again. The explosion was very loud. I fell to the floor."

The branch of the tree was tapping and scratching at the window. The candles flickered and then burned brightly again. The room grew warm.

"Did you see the woman's face, Benny?"

"No, she was wearing a veil. But she spoke with a man's voice, especially the second time she spoke."

"Do you think it was a man dressed as a woman?"

"Well, it could have been a woman...I..." he looked at Rosalinda and then back up at me and shrugged.

"Had you ever heard that voice before, Benny?" I asked.

"No sir"

I noticed Rosalinda move again. She had unbuttoned the top button of her robe and was unbuttoning the second button. I could see the beginning of the rise of her breasts. Then she buttoned up again.

I was getting ready to ask Benny another question when suddenly an image, quick and unbidden, jumped into my mind. I saw Rosalinda lying on the bed, smiling, her robe flung open, the glow of the candlelight upon her skin.... The image flashed by. I looked at Rosalinda's face. It seemed there was a hint of a wry smile. Had she seen something in my eyes? I looked at her again, but there was no smile.

"You know, Detective Q," she said, her voice quite cold, "Benito has given all this information to two other policemen."

I looked at Benny. "Please bear with me on this, Benny. I must hear your information from you."

"Yes," said Benny. "I don't mind."

"The woman," I said, "tall, short?"

"Tall, yes, tall for a woman."

"Afterward, did she leave right away?"

"Yes, a second or two later I heard the bell again."

Rosalinda moved again. "Really, Detective Q, you should—"

"Yes, Miss Lucero, I will certainly check with the other officers, but for now this must be done."

Rosalinda glared at me. I looked steadily back at her.

"Miss Lucero, did you run back from church by any chance?"

"Run? No. I walked quickly, you know, like sensible people do in the cold."

I ignored her sarcasm. "Did you see anyone leaving the store?" I asked.

Rosalinda turned her head to one side. She looked away from me for some time, as though she would much rather look at a bare wall than look at me. Finally, she spoke again. "I saw a woman, not running, walking on the other side of the street."

"Moving toward you or away from you?"

"Away from me, walking south on Campbell, and," she gave me the full impact of her glare, "before you ask, I have no idea what she was wearing."

"Thank you for saving me the trouble." I said. My words came quickly, despite my resolve to remain calm and professional. She seemed pleased with my irritation.

"What were you wearing, Miss Lucero?" Again, she did not respond right away. She was making me wait.

"This," she said, standing up to reveal a light brown wool dress draped over the chair, "and this." She lifted the dress to reveal a full-length green coat. Still standing, she said, "Is there anything else?" She was looking straight at me now. I matched her stare for a moment, then I looked away.

"Rose," Benny said as he went to her and stroked her arm. "Detective Quiñones has to ask us these questions. It's okay, Rose."

I saw the glistening of Rosalinda's eyes, and the look she gave her brother. It was a sad look, and full of love. I knew that she would never do anything to hurt him. She bent down and kissed him on the forehead.

Wanting to move past the situation, I said. "Benny, what grade are you in?"

"I am in the sixth grade."

"You are nine?" I asked, confused, since I thought that a nine year old should be in perhaps the fourth grade.

"He was promoted two grades." Rosalinda said.

Benny looked at me, slightly embarrassed at the obvious pride in Rosalinda's voice, and shrugged. I gave him a thumbs up. He gave me a hint of a smile. Sam was right. Little Benny had the manners and bearing of a grown up.

I was about to ask Rosalinda if she had come in through the store entrance, when the doorway curtain ruffled and blew in towards us. I heard the voice of Torres, coming in to the kitchen the same way that I had entered. He was laughing and joking with Sam. He knew I was in the bedroom.

"Yes sir. We have got it made, Sammy boy. You bet. *Simon, sin chingaderas.* Detective Q is going to solve this case in no time flat. Bet your ass. What this case needs is some young blood. Hell, me and Evan? We're just a couple of old farts. Don't know shit. Couldn't find our asses with both hands. But Detective Q? Now there's one smart detective. *Simon, ese.* I heard he scored one hundred and ten percent on that bitch of a test. Don't ask me how that's possible, that's just what I heard, *y otra cosa…*" He lowered his voice slightly and continued.

Torres had begun calling me Detective Q shortly after he came back into the department. It was intended to get my goat, I'm sure. He was the only person who called me that. That is, until tonight. Tonight, Rosalinda had called me that twice.

I glanced at Rosalinda. Her head was cocked toward the kitchen but there was otherwise no change to her demeanor. Benny had moved back to the bed. He stood up and walked over to the candles and looked down into the jars that held them. He moved to the window and opened the curtain. A thin branch screeched against the glass, moving back and forth in the wind. Benny moved back to the bed, sat on it, and with one finger hurriedly traced one of the squares in the quilt on the bed. All of his actions happened very quickly.

Torres' voice began to rise again and then abruptly stopped. I knew there could be only one explanation for his sudden silence. It meant that Evan had stepped into the room. I had seen how Torres carried on out of Evan's presence, but around Evan he was very different. It was obvious to me that he idolized Evan. Torres, also, was a sharp dresser. There was a subdued conversation, which I could not make out and then Evan stepped into the bedroom.

Evan's glance swept past me as he studied the room. He looked up toward the ceiling to the empty light fixture, to the window, to the candles, to Benny, and finally to Rosalinda.

Rosalinda spoke first. "Good evening, Detective Morrow. This is my brother, Benito."

"Young man." Evan said, bowing slightly.

For a moment, Benny sat motionless on the bed. Then he stood up and extended his hand. *"A sus ordenes,* Detective Morrow."

Evan spoke again. "My condolences to each of you. It is a shame. I am sorry to have to ask you any questions at a time like this but it must be done. I also apologize if I ask you to repeat any answer you may have previously given."

I looked at Rosalinda but she ignored me.

The curtain that hung at the doorway went a little more than three-quarters of the way to the floor. From my angle, to one side, I could see Torres' highly polished shoes. He was standing sideways, probably leaning against the wall.

Evan then moved quickly through a series of questions that he directed to Rosalinda but would frequently look at Benny during her answers. I made verbatim notes of each question and answer in shorthand.

The victim's last name was Benavidez. He had changed his last name to his mother's maiden name, Solares, at some point but Rosalinda was not sure when. He was 70 years old. He had been born in Torreon, Mexico. He had arrived in El Paso sometime in the early Twenties. Unlike the other three victims, he was not in the process of being naturalized. He was a legal resident. He would renew his residency each year as allowed by law according to his financial worth.

He had owned the grocery store since the late twenties. The store was open daily from 5:30 to 12:30, closed for two hours, and then open again from 2:30 until 10:00. On Thursdays, the store would not reopen after the 12:30 closure.

The victim, as far as Rosalinda knew, had never been married. He was not their uncle but their mother's cousin. They called him uncle because of his age and to show respect. The victim had taken in Rosalinda and Benny five years before at the time of the deaths of Rosalinda's father and mother. For some reason Evan did not ask how the parents had died.

Rosalinda said that the victim sometimes went across the bridge for lunch during the 12:30 to 2:30 closure times. Usually, on Thursdays he would leave promptly at 12:30 and not return until after midnight. Neither Rosalinda nor Benny knew where he went during those times.

Quite abruptly, Evan looked at me and said, "Detective Quiñones, I trust you have all the information you need here?" He smiled. This was not really a question. It was his indication to me that this particular session was over. It was my cue.

"Yes I have, Detective Morrow." I said, as I closed my notebook and placed it in my inner coat pocket.

Evan looked at Benny and asked, "By the way, young man, did you help your uncle install that new linoleum in the kitchen?"

"No sir, when I got home from school it was already there."

"When was that?"

"Last month, I think, on a Thursday."

As Benny answered, Evan glanced at Rosalinda, I assume to see if she would corroborate his answer. I glanced at her also in time to see her staring at me.

Evan was into his next question, "…would you know if your uncle fought in the revolution?"

Rosalinda's eyes moved quickly back to Evan. "He never mentioned that. No, I do not remember him ever speaking of that."

Evan said, "I bring that up only because of that photograph… on the refrigerator."

"Oh, that is mine. The two ladies in the photograph are my grandmother and my great-aunt."

Exactly, I thought, there was a definite resemblance between Rosalinda and the two ladies in the picture.

"Very beautiful ladies, I must say." Evan said.

"Thank you, Detective Morrow."

Evan bowed slightly toward Rosalinda and said, "Miss Lucero, I do not wish to alarm you and it is very probable that I am being overly cautious but I am concerned for you and your brother's safety. There is the possibility that the person who did this may return to do you some harm."

In one quick movement, Rosalinda moved from her chair to Benny's side on the bed. She held him tightly as she placed her face into the hair on his head. Evan continued, "Therefore, I am placing you and Benito in protective custody. A couple of days, maybe three. You are familiar with the holding center residence back behind the station?"

The residence in question was used mainly as a holding place for illegal Mexicans, usually women, charged with non-violent crimes awaiting deportation. It was a two-story structure that contained a number of small apartments.

"Yes," answered Rosalinda.

"Very well. Detective Quiñones and I will step out while you and Benito get ready."

Through the bottom of the curtain I saw Torres move quickly away. When Evan and I passed back out of the bedroom Torres was studying his face in the mirror above the kitchen sink.

"So what's the plan, Number One?" Torres said. I didn't know if Torres had always called Evan Number One. Maybe so. But in any event, and by extension, that would make me number two.

Evan replied, "For now, we need to get Miss Lucero and Benito down to the holding center."

Torres turned around and said, "Right, exactly. I'll drive them down right away."

Evan said, "No, Tommy. Sammy here will take them." Then to Sam, Evan said, "Sammy, bring your car around to the back. Get as close as you can to those oleanders out there. Walk back and escort Miss Lucero and Benito out. See if you can do this without anyone seeing them. You are to call me when you arrive."

Sam was already at the door putting on his coat. Evan looked back at Torres and continued. "Tommy, I need you to brief the reporters. Get a statement from each officer out there. Create a timeline and then brief the reporters. You know the routine."

Torres said, "Sure, right, Number One. Club of Clubs, right?"

"More or less," answered Evan, "for now the newspapers can call it that."

Torres smiled. "What's the deal, Number One?"

Evan removed a cigarette from his pack but did not light it. "Just a couple of things. For one, this victim was not in the process of becoming a citizen."

"And the other?" asked Torres.

Evan looked at his cigarette for a moment and then placed it back in the pack. "I'm not sure yet, Tommy."

Torres almost bumped into me, and would have if I had not moved, as he turned and headed towards the store area.

I waited for a moment or two and then I also walked out toward the store. I still hadn't seen the crime scene first hand. As I passed through the storage area, I noticed that the doors to the closet were open. There were some old, full-length dresses on hangers. I wondered whose they were, since they were certainly not something that Rosalinda might wear. I passed through the curtain that led to the living room. Benny's homework was still on the floor. I picked up all of the papers, arranged them as best I could, and inserted them behind the cover of an American History textbook. I went back through the storage area and into the kitchen. At that moment Benny, wearing a jacket, was coming out of the bedroom. Noticing his book and homework in my hand, he moved toward me and took them from me. Without looking at the sheets he said, "I think there is another sheet of paper underneath the sofa."

I followed Benny into the storage area and then he turned to me and whispered something. I bent down and he whispered again.

"Is that other detective an okay cop?"

"Detective Morrow?" I asked. "Most definitely."

"No, the other one. The one who doesn't like you."

I smiled to myself. This was a perceptive little guy. "You mean Torres?"

Benny asked again. "Yes, is he a good cop?" The question surprised me.

"I…well, yes, of course, Benny. But why do you ask such a thing?"

"I don't know. His voice…"

I heard Rosalinda in the kitchen. Her voice was loud and strained. "Where is Benito?"

"Here I am, Rose." Benny answered, as he hurried back into the kitchen.

Rosalinda held two small suitcases, one in each hand. She was wearing a green coat. She looked very pale. Sam opened the kitchen door and the three of them stepped out into the night.

I thought quickly. What had prompted Benny's question? What was it about Torres' voice? It was an ordinary voice. Arrogant perhaps, but otherwise...?

I told Evan that I needed to clarify a point as I walked out of the door. The wind had stopped gusting. Now it was steady. The three-quarter moon was directly overhead. Rosalinda and Benny were just approaching the oleanders as I called out. I walked up to them and advised Sam that Evan had further instructions.

"Yes?" He said.

"Detective Morrow said that no one is to contact these two."

"Right."

"He also said that you are to note and report to me anyone attempting to contact these two. That includes any member of the police department."

Sam looked at me, a surprised look on his face. "Very good." He answered.

"You two go ahead." I told him, indicating himself and Rosalinda. Rosalinda objected but I waved her off.

I stood with Benny as Sam and Rosalinda got into his police car.

"What did you mean back there, Benny?"

"I don't know, just asking." He was shivering and tugging on the zipper of his jacket, trying to get up as high as it would go.

"You're going to be okay, Benny. It will be warm down at the center. If you get hungry have Sam tell the cook there to fix you something."

"Okay."

"If you need or want to talk to me tell Sam to call me. Otherwise, I'll probably see you in the morning, okay?"

"Okay." Benny said, as he turned and walked quickly to the waiting car.

I watched the police car move down the street and then as I stepped forward to see it turn the corner I felt something soft brush against my ear. There was something stuck to one of the oleander branches. It had not been there before. I reached up and detached the article and shined my flashlight on it. It was a black lace veil. I put my nose to it and smelled it. Perfume, I thought. No, not perfume. After-shave lotion. Very distinctive. Yes, I knew it well. A knot materialized in the pit of my stomach as I placed the veil into the inside pocket of my overcoat.

4

I did not go back to the kitchen entrance. Instead, I walked out to the Campbell Street side and back around towards the store entrance. The crowd was gone, as were most of the cars. Torres and the reporters were gone also. I figured they had moved on to the "Blue Moon" bar and restaurant on Stanton Street, which was a late night gathering place for gamblers, prostitutes, crime reporters, and cops.

There was no one inside the store. It was narrow, maybe twelve feet wide by about twenty feet long. Half of the counter area was actually counter; the other half was a display cabinet with breads and pastries. To the left there was an opening to get behind the counter. There was no opening to the right. There were two curtained doorways. One led to the storage room, the other to the room where I had retrieved Benny's homework. Above that doorway was a framed painting that showed a mission church in the center of a small village with a shaft of sunlight striking the bell in the tower.

There were only three short steps from the door to the counter. The smooth, well-worn tin counter had a thin layer of fingerprint dust all around. The playing card was gone. I made a mental note that I should interview Octavio Ochoa regarding the playing card business. His articles sounded believable but for some reason I did not believe them. Maybe it was his style. There were men,

Mr. Ochoa said, who he called "*carteros*" (postmen) who were avenging something related to some treachery at the time of the attack on Columbus, New Mexico in 1916. The men who were being murdered he called "*bastos*" which in English is the suit of clubs in playing cards. Yes, I would definitely interview Mr. Ochoa but for now the victim held my attention.

The wind rattled the double doors at the entrance as I moved closer to the body. The victim's left arm rested on the counter. I could see the inky blackness of his fingertips where he had been fingerprinted. The little finger on his left hand was missing. The victim's skin was a grayish color. The eyes, still open, had now filmed over. The victim was bald except for a downy wisp of white hair on each side just above the ears. His face was round and smooth. Very smooth. Aside from his thin eyebrows, the victim had no facial hair whatsoever.

I walked around the counter and behind the body. The cash register was open, there was money in it. There were two empty pop bottles next to the cash register. In the mouth of one of the bottles there was a tightly folded empty cigarette pack. Behind the victim, to his left, was a cigarette rack. The victim was sitting on a stool with wheels on it. There was a long pool of dark blood on the floor along the bottom of the counter and there was a blood-soaked newspaper propped up between the stool and the counter. It was the Juarez newspaper, "*El Grito*." Toward the back of his neck, slightly down from his right ear, the victim had a strawberry birthmark, triangular in shape, which looked now to be the color of fresh blood. The victim was wearing a threadbare navy-blue sweater. His right hand almost touched the newspaper. He was narrow shouldered but thick in the middle. His buttocks hung over the stool. A blue bandanna type handkerchief stuck half way out of his back pocket. He was wearing gray gabardine pants, also quite worn. His left foot was flat on the floor; his right foot was up, with only the toes touching the floor. He was wearing huaraches over thick gray socks.

I stepped back through the curtain and sat on the sofa in the living room. I moved around until I found the spot where Benny would have had to be sitting in order to see the killer. I found the spot. There were probably only eight paces and a partially open curtain, separating killer from witness. The knot in my stomach moved. Had the killer seen Benny? Probably not, I decided. The store was very brightly lit. The only illumination in the living room was a small, green-shaded table lamp next to a telephone. Benny had said that he had seen the killer through a narrow slit in the curtain. I took out the black lace veil from my pocket and smelled it again. The scent was unmistakable. It was "Barrington's Blue Cross." I had used that same after-shave lotion myself until it had begun to irritate my skin.

As I was sitting on the sofa making notes, I heard the bell above the store entrance ring. I could see the coroner and two officers carrying a stretcher. The coroner had a white sheet draped over his arm. Through the slit I watched as the two officers lowered the body to the floor and placed it on the stretcher and covered it with the white sheet. I heard them carry it back around the counter. I heard the bell again and then they were gone.

I did not move from the sofa. Thoughts of Rosalinda began to inch up into the corners of my mind. It did not take long for those thoughts to crowd everything else out. *Detective.* She had stressed the word because she was the one who had helped me celebrate my promotion.

I was not sure how I felt. There was regret on my part, for sure, but there was also something else and I was not quite certain what it was. I had met Rosalinda before I met Penny. The attraction was mutual, the affair moved quickly. Shortly after I met Penny I had broken it off with Rosalinda. Then, during the time that Penny and I had separated and on the day of my promotion to detective, a group of the guys at the station had suggested that we all get together with our wives or girlfriends and go to Juarez to celebrate. We were to meet at the Stanton Street Bridge at seven in the evening. I did not want to go alone so I had asked Rosalinda to go with me. Smiling and arching an eyebrow, Rosalinda had said, "Well now, what's taken you so long?"

It was dark and chilly by the time I got to the bridge. The party group had gone ahead but Rosalinda had waited for me. She was wearing a red blazer over a black vest with a white blouse and a gray tight skirt. She was wearing gloves the exact shade of gray as her skirt. As we were walking across the bridge, I saw Penny coming back on the opposite side. She was walking alongside her friend and fellow teacher, Josie, from Bowie High School. Behind them were two young men I did not recognize. Penny was smiling. One of the young men said something and she turned and laughed. They were all laughing together. Penny had not seen me. At that moment, Rosalinda slipped her arm through mine as we continued across the bridge. Then we were in Mexico.

We had worked our way from nightclub to nightclub and finally ended up at the "Del Rio." I had been drinking rum and cola doubles. Rosalinda was wearing an intoxicating perfume. As we danced, I whispered in her ear, "Rosalinda, you are indeed a lovely rose." She laughed and pressed closer. Her lips brushed lightly on my neck. I asked her if she wanted to go to the Christmas Party with me. She said, "What do you think?" I said I thought we might be thinking the same thing. She said she was certain of it.

That night, my telephone was ringing when I got back to my apartment at 2:00 in morning. It was Penny. We talked for a long while, each apologizing to the other. The break up had been over nothing really. A foolish thing. And as I thought about it it was almost like a contest to see just how stubborn I could be. Penny asked me to move back, and I agreed. We had been apart for three weeks. I showered and dressed and went to work.

At work I walked over to Rosalinda's section and asked her if she would have coffee with me at her first break in the cafeteria across the street from the station. She looked very good. She looked radiant. I felt bad.

Rosalinda made her entrance into the cafeteria. She was smiling and laughing, exchanging banter with her friends sitting at tables along the way. She seemed a little breathless as she sat down. I told her that I was very, very sorry but that I was moving back with my wife. She looked into my eyes with a confused look that lasted a fraction of a second. She laughed a short, dry laugh. I said, "I am sorry, Rosalinda." Her voice had a tone that I had never heard before. Hate, on ice. "Oh, but I can assure you," she said, "that it is quite all right."

She stood up quickly and leaned over me with one hand on the table. I was frozen by her glare. I thought she was going to say something else but she didn't. What she did do was with her other hand she deliberately slid my cup of coffee onto my lap.

Rosalinda had not spoken to me again, until tonight.

5

When I got back to the kitchen, Evan had moved the table and chairs toward the bedroom. He was rolling the linoleum back to expose the wood slats of the flooring. I helped him move the refrigerator toward the door. Neither of us spoke. In the middle of the room, over which the table had been, there was a cut out rectangle of about two feet by two-and-a-half feet. Evan lifted out that section to reveal a hole in the ground in which sat an old wood and metal trunk. We lifted it out and set it to the side. It had a rusty open lock in its hasp. Evan removed the lock and opened the trunk. It was empty. I was disappointed but Evan seemed pleased.

The inside of the trunk was lined with a tattered canvas-type material. Evan ran his fingers all along the cloth until he found something. He worked the object up with his fingers toward a tear in the material near the top. He moved his hand back down and pulled up another object. He held them in the palm of his hand. Evan made a sound in his throat and handed two Mexican gold coins to me. They were shiny; they felt smooth and hefty. The date on them was 1910.

We replaced the trunk in the hole and placed the cut out section over it. We unrolled the linoleum back over the slats and moved the table and chairs back. I eased the refrigerator back into position. Evan sat at the table and lit a cigarette. He placed the two shiny coins side by side in the middle of the table. I was about to ask him how he knew to look for the trunk and what connection an empty, or almost empty, trunk had on this homicide when he spoke.

"I knew this victim." I waited as Evan exhaled a long stream of smoke toward the ceiling. "Although when I knew him," Evan thought a moment, "years ago, in Arizona, he was posing as a woman by the name of Doña Fortuna. He fooled everyone in Santa Rosa." Evan paused, flicking the ashes from his cigarette into the ashtray. "Santa Rosa," he repeated the name slowly, "was a mile-high mining town at the end of the world."

Evan looked at me and smiled at the expression on my face. His was a sad smile. For a moment, perhaps it was the angle of the light, he appeared much older than his years.

Evan continued. "I believe that Doña Fortuna killed my father. In 1920, with my own eyes, I saw her kill the man from Mexico who had been sent to kill her. I ran away from home then. I was later adopted, changed my name…"

Evan stopped. He was looking at the picture of Pancho Villa. My mind was struggling with the information he had just given me. I was trying to phrase my questions to him when the telephone in the living room rang. I walked quickly to the telephone, assuming it was Sam calling me to let me know that he had arrived at the holding center. I answered the telephone with a question. "Hey Sam, did you make it okay?"

"What? No, it's Bellamy. Who's this?"

"I'm sorry, Bellamy, this is Vince."

"Hey, Vince. Evan wanted me to let him know right away."

"Yes?"

"The card has no prints, unlike the others."

"Okay."

"Yeah, no prints on this one but tell Evan his hunch was right about the other three."

"How's that?"

"We've got a match between the deceased's fingerprints and the prints on the other three cards."

"Are you sure, Bellamy?"

Bellamy laughed. "Come on, Vince. What's wrong, can't you take good news?"

"Sorry, man." I said. "It seems like a lot has happened. Didn't mean to doubt you."

"That's okay, Vince. Tell Evan he owes me a cold one. Check that, it's too damn cold for a cold one. Make that a coffee royal."

"Right, Bellamy. Thanks."

I put the telephone back on the cradle and turned to go back to the kitchen when it rang again. This time it was Sam. They had arrived okay. Rosalinda and Benny had gone straight to bed, he said. I reminded him to stay on duty until he could be relieved in the morning.

I walked back to the kitchen and relayed Bellamy's information to Evan.

He looked away and seemed distracted for a moment, as though he had not heard me. Then he spoke in a softer and lower voice. "So, now we know who killed the other three."

I said, "This victim was a *cartero?*"

"No, Vinny, he was the leader of the Club of Clubs."

This was the first time that I had heard Evan use that term. For some reason, I had been under the impression that he did not believe Mr. Ochoa's articles.

"I thought…" I began, but Evan had read my mind.

"In general, Octavio had it right. But in the specifics he did not."

I waited for Evan to continue but he was looking at the photograph on top of the refrigerator again.

I spoke. "Evan, this man was a *basto* then?"

"Yes."

"And he was killing his own friends?"

"Correct."

"Was it for money?"

"It was to silence them, no doubt. I believe he thought that once they became United States citizens their allegiance to him would evaporate."

Evan's voice regained its usual strength. "He, on the other hand, this Faustino Benavidez, who called himself Maximo Solares and who used to be Doña Fortuna, *was* killed for his money. I don't know how much money was left in that trunk, but at one time there could have been up to $70,000 in Mexican gold coin and bank notes."

"So," I said, "a *cartero* killed him?"

"No, Vinny, I do not think so. I cannot say for sure now but if it had been a *cartero*, I think that the card would have been the queen of clubs."

Evan stood up and put on his overcoat. He removed an envelope from one of his pockets and placed the coins inside and sealed it. I put on my coat and followed Evan into the living room. He walked to the telephone and dialed a number.

"Jake? Evan. Yes, thank you for your quick work. Right, exactly. Well, sometimes a guy gets lucky, you know. Listen. Yes, yes. Listen, Jake. The information is between us for now, okay? I appreciate it. That's right. Yes, there is. Is the victim's pistol in your possession? Okay. I need you to run the test on that pistol to see if those bullets match the bullets removed from the other three. I would like corroboration for the fingerprint match. Very good, Jake. Good night."

Evan and I walked out of the store. He walked over to one of the police cars parked off in the shadows and spoke to the officer. He came back to me and said, "Okay, Vinny. I'm leaving a couple of men here." He looked at me and said, "You okay, Vinny?"

"Yes, sure, it's just that…"

"A lot of stuff, right?"

"Yes" I said. *A hell of a lot of stuff,* I thought.

"Things are looking up, Vinny. I'm confident that we have the other three out of the way."

Evan seemed at peace and excited at the same time. I was not ready to tell him what Benny had asked me nor about the veil that was not there when I first walked by the oleanders and then was there when I had walked back out, and that as far as I knew the only other person who had been by there was Torres. In the stinging cold wind my concerns seemed of no substance.

Evan said, "I'm going to spend the night across the river. You have Graciela's number over there?"

Graciela was Evan's lady friend. She was a tall, attractive woman. They said she was rich.

"Yes" I said.

"Okay, Vinny. Goodnight, see you in the morning."

I drove home. It was 2:30 am. I undressed quietly and set my alarm for 6:00. I got into bed and felt the warmth of Penny's body as she pressed up against my back. She murmured, "Home?"

"Yes," I said, and fell into a deep sleep.

6

In the morning Penny was up before me. I could smell the coffee. I shaved, showered, and dressed quickly.

Penny was in the kitchen. There was a neat stack of graded papers on the table. She had the newspaper in her hands. The headline read, "Club of Clubs Strikes Again!" with a string of "EXTRAS" across the top of the page. There was a picture that showed the front of the store and Evan walking towards it. I was blocked out since I was walking beside him but on the tenement side. The caption read simply: "Detective Morrow approaches the crime scene at 9th and Campbell."

I bent down and kissed Penny on the cheek. "Good morning."

Penny smiled. "Good morning." She poured some cream into my cup of coffee. "Vince, there is no mention of you anywhere in this article."

I laughed. "I'll give you three guesses as to the source for the article."

"Torres?"

I laughed again. Penny had met Torres and was not quite sure how to take him. When I had asked her what she thought of him, she had responded that she was not sure. Then she had added, "Well, for one thing, he is too pretty. Can't trust a pretty man." For a moment I considered voicing my concerns about Torres. I decided against it. My suspicions seemed perverse to me somehow. Instead,

I told Penny about the crime scene and how the victim looked with his black fingertips. I told her about Rosalinda, not about the past of course, but the rest of it and about Benny. Penny pushed the newspaper away. Her eyes told me to go on.

"There was trunk buried beneath the floor boards of the kitchen." I said.

"Really?"

"Yes, it contained two gold coins." I said. Penny's eyes lit up.

I rehearsed what Evan had said in my mind. I had still not thoroughly digested what he had told me. Penny began tapping her fingers on the table. "Yes? And?"

"Well, Evan said that at one time that trunk held maybe 70,000 dollars in gold coin and bank notes. And that the victim had been posing as a woman in some small mining town in Arizona where he, Evan, was from."

"Say again?" Penny said.

I repeated my statement. A small frown appeared on Penny's face. "Evan knew the victim?"

"Yes, as a boy. He said that this victim had probably killed his father…"

A small gasp came from Penny's mouth. "Killed his father?"

"Yes, and that another man, a man from Mexico, was sent to kill him but that he, or she, at the time, had killed that man also."

Penny held up her hand, an indication for me to slow down or stop. She took a sip of her coffee. Then she said, "Whoa. You are saying that this victim was posing as a woman? And all this happened in Arizona?"

"Yes, Penny. And I got the impression that Evan witnessed the second murder."

"Oh my. Evan went through all of this as a boy?"

"Yes. But that was not his real name. He was ten or eleven years old when he ran away from home."

"And Evan had never told you any of this before?"

"No. But I really don't think that that would be something that he would want to discuss."

"I should say so." Penny paused and took another sip of her coffee. "But how very interesting, Vin."

"Actually strange, Penny, and what is stranger still is that Evan is pretty sure that this victim was the perpetrator of the other so-called Club of Club's murders."

As Penny fixed us some toast and a cheese omelet, I went back and filled in some of the details as they came back to me. When I was finished, Penny turned from the stove and said, "That is a most fascinating story, Vince." She had the look in her eyes that she always got when I was involved in an interesting case. That is to say that my wife was enthralled.

Penny loved crime, at a distance of course. In the abstract. She loved the search for clues. She had a knack for connecting things that had no apparent connection. Crime, as an idea, excited her. She had the mind of a sleuth but she had no stomach for the actual thing itself. I believed that if she were to see a murder scene, in all its grotesqueness, she would faint. I had tried to tell her one night, how, when one first sees the victim the mind recoils, and, if it has been long enough, one's sense of smell is overwhelmed. And still, I had said to her, if one can overcome that first sensory bombardment, there is an aura about the body. Something that cannot be named adequately. It is an echo or vibration of the victim's last moan or gasp or cry for help.

My words had frightened Penny. We had been lying in bed and she had placed her hand over my mouth. She had begun to tremble and laughed a long nervous laugh. She said she was reminded of a story her grandfather told her and her cousins when they were children. He would tell it on cold winter nights and was always adding to it. He would change his voice to accommodate each character. The children would beg him to tell it and then scream and run around looking for a place to hide when he would lower his voice and begin.

In the village of Cerca de Nunca (near to never), he would say, there lived two men, Pedro and Jose, who were rival suitors for the hand of the beautiful Maria Nunca Cerca (never near). She liked them both but could not decide which one to marry. One night, Pedro enticed Jose out into his pumpkin patch to help him dig a hole where he said a witch had told him a sack of gold was buried. After the hole was dug, Pedro hit Jose over the head with his shovel and buried him. Here, according to Penny, her grandfather would imitate the impact of being hit on the back of the head with a shovel. That is, his head would drop forcefully down to his chest. Then, ever so slowly, he would begin to raise his head with his eyes closed and keep them closed for a few moments. This, of course, would drive the children into fits of hysteria until the grandmother would come into the room and tell the grandfather to quit his foolishness, which he would half do. That is, he would keep one eye open and the other closed as he told the children how the villagers looked high and low for Jose for two weeks to no avail. The beautiful Maria cried every day for her beloved Jose because death, of course, makes every man taller and handsomer and kinder in the memory of the living.

The next fall, at harvest time, there was one particularly large pumpkin in the middle of the field. When that pumpkin was cut from the vine and turned over, it was noticed that some dirt had caked into small fissures on the underside of the pumpkin in the form of letters, and the letters spelled the words: "Pedro killed me." Now, I smiled at Penny's story.

Penny and I got ready to leave. We agreed that I would pick her up for lunch at noon. As Penny collected all of her papers she said, "Bellamy said there were no prints on the card?"

"Right, Penny."

"And only he and Evan and you knew this?"

"Yes, why?"

"Well, how did Torres know there were no prints?"

"What do you mean?"

"In the article he is quoted as saying there were no prints on the card."

I glanced through the article. Penny was right.

7

On the way to the high school Penny asked me if I thought that the victim would have been able to move the furniture and install the linoleum by himself. I said no. The victim was of a slight build, and old.

"In that case, Vince, I would be interested to find out who helped him. Whoever that person was must have noticed the cut out section on the wood floor, don't you think?"

"Yes, it was pretty obvious." I said.

We drove in silence for a while and then Penny spoke again.

"Vince?"

"Yes?"

"This is a strange case isn't it?"

"Yes it is, Penny."

"I mean," said Penny, "there was no robbery at the time of the murder, right?"

"Correct."

"So, why would you rob someone on one day and then come back and kill him on another? I mean, you've got the money. Why go back?"

"I don't know, Penny." I said. "At least not yet."

"Unless," Penny spoke softly, almost to herself, "you know that the person you have robbed is going to find out you, and only you, could have done it…"

We drove a while longer and then Penny said. "Oh!"

"Have you solved it, Penny?" I asked, only half-jokingly.

"No. I think I'm getting a headache over this. There is no writing on this pumpkin, right?" We laughed together.

Penny continued to speak of the case. I tuned her in and out. There was much on my mind.

"...so, for sure there was gold in the trunk, right? I mean, who would re-bury an empty trunk? But, and here is the part that gives me a headache, Vince, why come back? Unless what you've got are two separate, unrelated crimes. One guy robs him and someone else kills him. Do you suppose these are two unrelated crimes?" I considered that possibility but I did not answer.

"But wait," said Penny, "maybe we're getting ahead of ourselves here." I chuckled. It was funny to me how Penny took possession of a case. She spoke as though it was her homicide. I was her assistant.

"Let me see here," she said, "this victim was the leader of the *bastos*. He had some power over them. He's about to lose that power so he starts to plug them." I laughed at Penny's choice of words.

"Please, Penny."

Catching my laughter, Penny began speaking in a movie gangster voice. She did a very good Edward G. Robinson impression. "Yeah, that's right, well, yes, I see. Hmmmm. The first victim is easy, pal. Yeah, sure, nothing to it. He has no idea." Penny removed an imaginary cigar from her mouth and blew imaginary smoke upward. "The second victim, well, that's a different story see? The leader says to him, we better stick close together tonight pal, you know, it's the fifth, yeah, and the *carteros* are on to us. Be sure all your loved ones are out of the house, wouldn't want them to get hurt would we? Well, there you go and bang, two down. So sorry, my friend, gotta go. Got an appointment next month same night, same time. Yeah."

Penny kept talking but I was thinking of Evan. Why had he not followed up on the question about the linoleum? Was he slipping perhaps? But then again how would I act in that same situation? Could I investigate the homicide of the man who had killed my father? Evan had not been himself. I had noticed it in his car. Maybe it had been the flashing of the police car lights but it had seemed to me that I had seen Evan's hand shake when he brought the cigarette up to his mouth.

I put those thoughts out of my mind and instead concentrated on what I knew, which was that someone had walked into that grocery store and shot a man in the chest and walked back out. There was a dead man with a strange and homicidal past. Nothing taken but a card is left behind. And, according to Evan, the wrong card at that. Now, out of a hundred questions, the first one in my mind was who? Who would just walk in, say a few insignificant words, and shoot? A man dresses up as a woman and kills another man who used to dress up as a woman. What did that mean? That was my second question.

"So," Penny was saying, "you'll pick me up for lunch?"

We were suddenly at the school. "Yes, at noon." I said.

"Tell me everything you find out." She called back as she walked away from the car.

I watched Penny walk away. Overhead, thick gray clouds threatened rain.

8

I drove away from the high school and past the murder scene and then on to the police station. I remembered that I still had the veil in my overcoat pocket. It no longer had the scent. I took out a large evidence envelope from my desk and wrote my initials and badge number plus the time and location of the discovery. I put a note inside along with the veil stating that at the time of discovery the scent had been "Barrington's." I sealed the envelope and turned it in to the evidence room sergeant.

I walked out and walked across the long empty lot behind the station to the holding center residence and found Sam still on the job.

"Morning, Sam. No relief yet?"

"Yeah, Vince. Jarvis is on the way. Should be here any minute."

"Good. Any visitors last night?"

"None."

"Any calls?"

"Nope. No calls coming in. But an hour or so after they had gone to bed I heard Miss Lucero talking on the telephone in the hall with someone. She must've called out."

"Any idea who she was talking to?"

"I asked her this morning. She said it was one of her girl friends."

"By any chance, Sam, did she sound upset while she was on the telephone?"

"Couldn't tell. Speaking real low. I may have dozed off over there in that chair."

I glanced at the chair near the entrance and then to the telephone, which was just at the top of the stairs. It was about thirty feet.

"Is the boy up?" I asked.

"Yes, had breakfast and everything."

At that moment, Benny came walking down the stairs. He was clean faced; his hair was still wet and neatly parted.

"Good morning, Benny. How's it going?"

"Very good thank you, Detective Quiñones. What took you?"

I laughed. "Well, I had to drop off my wife at the school and all that, you know?"

"Okay," he said, "is she a teacher?"

"Yes, she teaches history at Bowie High."

Benny was now down at the bottom of the stairs and he walked over and shook my hand. "I'll be going to Bowie in a couple of years. I hope I get her."

"She'll be waiting for you I'm sure, Benny."

I led Benny away from Sam to a sofa at the opposite side of the lobby. I asked him if he had anything else to tell me about the night before.

"No. I think I was just scared. I'm okay now."

I looked down at his face. He was a good-looking little guy, bright and personable. I could not bear to tell him that his uncle had murdered those three other men. Eventually he would have to know, but I did not want to be the one to tell him.

"Benny" I said, "how is your sister this morning?"

"Very sad." He said.

"Benny" I said, "you understand that it is a detective's duty to ask questions?"

"Yes. You've got to find out everything if you want to solve a crime."

"Right, and if we are to solve a particular crime we need to know as much background as possible of all the people surrounding the crime."

"You are gathering facts?"

"Yes, exactly, Benny. And each fact is important."

"And a fact can lead you to the person who did this?"

"Exactly." I said again as I tried to phrase my next question. I did not want to upset him.

"Benny?"

"Yes?"

"Benny, this is important. Rosalinda, does she have a boyfriend?"

Benny thought for a moment. "No, not that I know of. A while back she said she really liked some guy but then she never mentioned it again." Benny removed his handkerchief from his pocket and rubbed it against a spot on the knee of his pants.

"Does anyone, a man perhaps, call her on the telephone?" I asked.

"Not that I know of. She does go out, sometimes during the week, but it's with her girlfriends." It occurred to me then that during the time that Rosalinda and I had dated I had always picked her up and dropped her off at a friend's house on Seventh. Benny was being truthful. He wanted to help. Still, he was careful when answering questions about his sister. I continued.

"Benny, were you aware that there was a trunk buried underneath your kitchen floor?"

"A trunk? With money? How much?" His questions were in quick succession. The excitement of buried treasure was in his eyes.

"You did not know?" I asked.

"No, but…"

I went on. "Do you remember anything about that day when the linoleum in your kitchen was replaced?" Benny thought for a moment. He was eager to answer my question. He was trying to remember everything.

"Well, I was at school. I'm pretty sure it was a Thursday. Usually, Uncle would be gone when I got home from school. He went across the river every Thursday and came back late, usually after I was in bed. But that day he was there and the new linoleum was down and Rose came out of the bedroom, she had stayed home that day because she wasn't feeling well. She fixed supper early for Uncle Maximo and me then she went back to bed."

"Rosalinda was not feeling well that day?"

"Yes, she was at home. I remember that her slippers made a squeaking sound as she moved across the new floor."

"Was the man who helped your uncle with the floor still there when you got home from school, Benny?" I asked the question casually, as though I knew that someone had helped his uncle.

"Yes, he was just leaving."

"Do you know this man?"

"They call him Vesuvio. He lives across the river. He is a deaf-mute."

I knew Vesuvio. He was a short but massive man; deaf, mute, and simple minded. They said he lived in a tin shack at the end of Mariscal Street. Every day except Sundays he would stand on the Mexican side of the bridge waiting for work. People would hire him to move furniture. He was a man of extraordinary strength. I myself had seen him walking up Virginia Street with a refrigerator strapped to his back. He seemed to enjoy doing it. The heavier the load, the broader his smile. I could exclude him as a suspect. He did not have the temperament for murder. Besides, if he ever did decide to kill someone he would not need a gun.

"Thank you, Benny. You know, last night, I didn't get a chance to ask about your parents."

"They died when I was four years old. Sometimes I can remember them, but other times I can't."

"I am sorry, Benny."

"They were killed in a train wreck. They were on their way back from a funeral in Chihuahua when the train derailed. Many other people were killed."

"Again, my condolences, Benny. So, at that time you came to live with your uncle?"

"Yes, I think so. My first memory of the store is of standing by the canal. I remember how the sunlight sparkled on the water." For a moment Benny's eyes had a faraway look. I waited a bit before continuing.

"Did you and Rosalinda get along with your uncle?"

"He was okay with me but he was very strict with her."

Benny's eyes became distant again. "Rose said that she was going to save her money and buy us a house way up on Montana Street. She said that we used to live up there when mother and father were alive. She said father was a brick mason. He built that house for us. We had a garden with flowers and fruit trees."

"That is the area where Mrs. Quiñones and I live, Benny. Maybe we can be neighbors someday."

"I would like that, Detective Quiñones." Benny smiled.

"Well then, Benny, I've got to move on. There is a lot to do. Thank you for your information."

I did not want to interview Rosalinda at this time. I would need to, I knew, but the moment did not seem right. I extended my hand and Benny shook it. He turned to walk up the stairs and stopped and turned back to me.

"Detective Quiñones, do you think my uncle was killed for his money?"

"Yes, I would say that could be a motive, Benny."

"But the killer left right away. I saw him walk in, shoot his pistol, and leave. He did not go into the kitchen."

"Benny, I think that perhaps the money had been taken before." Immediately, I regretted my words. There was a sudden look of alarm in Benny's eyes.

"So this…this thing that happened had nothing to do with the Club of Clubs?"

"Again, Benny…"

"And the killer was trying to trick you?"

I did not answer. I was amazed at Benny's very quick and alert mind. I smiled and nodded my head in time to see Rosalinda appear at the top of the stairs. There were dark lines under her eyes.

I called up to her. "Good morning, Miss Lucero." She did not look at me.

"Benito" she said, "I need you up here."

9

I walked around to the front entrance of the police station. Evan was standing on the steps with a crowd of people below him who were shouting questions at him. Evan was fielding all questions smoothly, in both Spanish and English. I walked over and stood off to one side.

As I watched the proceedings I remembered an article I had read about Evan in the Sunday newspaper while I was stationed at Fort Bliss. It was a lengthy interview with El Paso's most successful homicide detective. The writer of the article had written highly of Evan, saying that he was a legend in his own time.

The article moved me; it made me want to go into law enforcement. My own father had been a policeman. He was killed in the line of duty when I was very young and I had always had mixed emotions about police work but that article tipped the scales. I never mentioned this to Evan but my dream of becoming a homicide detective began on that day. The article took up several full pages of print, which I cut out and saved. There was a picture of Evan sitting at his desk, in vest and tie.

The article mentioned some of Evan's most famous cases including one in which the daughter of a state senator had been raped and murdered behind a drugstore in downtown El Paso. The article said that Evan had secured a confession from the girl's boyfriend, a member of one of El Paso's most prominent families, not at the police station, but over drinks at the Manhattan Bar in Juarez. When Evan was asked how he had been able to get a confession in that very troublesome case (there was much conflicting evidence indicating, perhaps, sex play gone wrong) he was quoted as saying, "When that young man told me that he had not raped her, I believed him." I had heard some suspects say that they would surrender to Evan only, and would shoot to kill anyone else who tried to arrest them.

Shortly after reading that article, I saw Evan in person for the first time. I was standing at a bus stop on Magoffin waiting for the bus back to the base when I saw a shiny new black Buick moving slowly down the street toward me. It made no sound. I saw the driver's face in the glow of the dashboard as he glided by. He was alone. A young boy standing close by looked up at me and smiled. He said, "Hey man, there goes Detective Evan Morrow. Looking for murder." The car came to a stop fifty feet or so past the bus stop. Evan stepped out wearing a gray suit with a light blue vest and a gray and blue tie. He waited by the side of his car, looking down the street away from us. The back door to the house he was looking at suddenly flew open and a man came running out. The man was wearing pajama bottoms and an undershirt. He was barefooted. He jumped over the picket fence and came running down the sidewalk crouched down and looking back toward the house. Evan moved out to the middle of the sidewalk and then the man saw him and stopped. Evan opened his coat on the left side. I assumed it was to show the man his badge or maybe the gun in his shoulder holster. The man smiled sheepishly and approached Evan with his hands up. Evan said something and the man leaned over the hood of the car and Evan frisked him in two long sweeping movements. He handcuffed the man with his hands behind his back, helped him into the back seat of the car, and drove off. The boy snapped his fingers and said, "Just like that!"

My attention was drawn back to the briefing. Evan was making a statement. "...fingerprints taken from last night's victim match the prints on each of the other three cards. In addition, the markings of the bullet test fired from the victim's pistol, which was found in a drawer beneath the counter at the crime scene, match the markings on the bullets removed from the other three victims." Evan paused for a moment. "We are confident, therefore, that this victim, acting alone, was the perpetrator of the other three murders and we will be closing those cases today."

Among the competing voices of the reporters was the question: "Isn't it unusual to fingerprint the victim?""

Evan answered quickly. "It is not unusual in the least."

As Evan was answering that question, another rang out: "In view of the fact that Detective Torres has said that there were no fingerprints on the card last night, does that mean you have no leads on this latest homicide?""

I focused on Evan's face. There was no change to his expression nor did he skip a beat. He looked at the reporter who had asked the question and said: "I trust you quoted Detective Torres accurately, Phil." Then he smiled.

"Gentlemen, regarding the status of any other leads, I am sorry but I cannot discuss the direction of our investigation at this time." Evan then thanked the reporters and turned to walk up the steps. A reporter who had a card sticking up out of his breast pocket that said "Dallas Bugle" called out, "Do you people have any idea what the motive might be in all these murders?""

For the briefest moment, I saw the irritation in Evan's face but when he turned back to address the reporter it was gone. In the same tone as the rest of the briefing, Evan said: "On occasion, motive is an invention by the people in your profession, sir. However, you should know that some individuals just like to kill."

As Evan continued up the steps and into the station, Octavio Ochoa came up to me and said, "I would like to speak to you, one on one, Detective Quiñones. Will you have coffee with me down the street?"

"Yes, sure." I said. Evan's response to the reporter regarding accuracy had given me pause. Suppose Torres had not said there were no prints? I needed to find out. I told one of the officers standing by to inform Evan that I would be down at "Nelo's" if he needed me.

10

Mr. Ochoa and I walked down the street to the café together. We sat down at a table by the window looking out toward the bus station. The waitress came by and Mr. Ochoa ordered a large breakfast while I ordered coffee.

"Congratulations on solving the other three cases, Detective Quiñones, or may I call you Vince?"

I had had nothing to do with solving the other three cases. He was congratulating me to flatter me, I suspected. His voice was smooth, his English perfect. His breath smelled faintly of alcohol. Although I had observed the dialogue between reporter and policeman, I had never spoken to a reporter one on one. They always went for Evan. But Mr. Ochoa had asked me to coffee and that in itself was a compliment in a way, I thought. I wondered if this would be an open, straightforward conversation or if he would choose to play word games like some reporters took pleasure in playing. I was alert and confident.

"By all means, call me Vince." I said.

"Good, good," he said, "and you may call me Octavio, please." He paused. "Unless you prefer Mr. Eighty-Eight."

He laughed. It was a short laugh without pleasure. Almost like three quick coughs. I could not be sure how he felt about the nickname that some at the station called him. Perhaps he had thrown it out to see my reaction. I smiled at him.

He said, "I have a confession to make to you, Vince." His dark hair, freshly cut, was combed straight back. He ran his hand through it. On one finger was a very large gold signet ring.

I decided to test him. "Your writing is not criminal, Octavio."

This laugh was deep and loud. I realized then that he had been nervous about me for some reason.

"Some people might disagree with you on that point." He said and laughed again. This time I laughed with him. The waitress brought our order, gave us each a smile and walked away.

"No, Vince, my confession is that I was not the first person to write about the Club of Clubs." I took a sip of my coffee as he continued.

"It was a small book written in Spanish purportedly by an American by the name of C. X. O'Brien. The book has a short biographical statement about the author. It said that he was an expatriate, as I recall, living in Mexico City. The book had been printed privately, I believe. The title of the book was *El Club de Bastos*. The word *club* means the same in Spanish as it does in English, that is, a group, but it is pronounced differently. The Spanish word, *bastos*, is the name for the suit of clubs in playing cards. Therefore, the title would translate into 'The Club of Clubs'." Octavio spread out his napkin and placed it on his lap.

"The dedication in the book was to the initials 'J. B.' and the date was November 1925. One day I received the book in my office at the newspaper. No note, no address. Just the book in a large envelope. I must admit that the book grabbed my interest from the first page. First of all because of the content but also because I could almost bet that it had been written by a woman. I thought to myself that if the writer would take such pains to conceal her identity then there must be some truth to what she was saying."

Octavio had my attention. I watched as he took a large forkful of scrambled eggs and potatoes, chewed quickly, took another, and then took a long swallow of hot coffee. He took two slices of crisp bacon and wrapped them in a still steaming corn tortilla and ate that. He was a deft and efficient eater.

"One day, when I had nothing really to write about," he looked at me with a sly smile, "and I was quite hungover, I wrote a piece. A filler, really, nothing more."

"And this was?" I asked.

"I would say that I received the book in late 1949. I wrote the article in the spring of the next year." Octavio thought for a moment and then nodded his head in confirmation. He ate a few more mouthfuls and then continued.

"I lent the book to Evan after the first murder. He reads very fast, as you must know. He read it in one sitting as we had lunch one day. You look surprised, Vince. You were not aware, perhaps, that Evan and I go way back?"

"No, I was not aware." I said, surprised.

"We were classmates and friends in high school." Octavio seemed to wait for that to sink in as he ate some more of his breakfast. "Someday, perhaps, you would be interested to hear about some of our adventures back then." Octavio looked into my eyes. "But no, perhaps not." He said.

"Yes," I said, "I think I would."

"You humor this old *vato*, Vincent. But I will say that Evan was a straight "A" student and an exceptional athlete. In algebra class, on many an occasion, I saw him complete the homework problems even as the teacher was assigning them." Octavio looked at me as though he wanted to say something else, changed his mind, and then seemed to change it back. "Evan was very popular, had more than a few girlfriends, but there was one that he particularly liked.

He and I pursued that same young girl during and after high school. She chose him, and they had a huge wedding. I was happy for them. Six months later she was killed in a car accident on her way to Las Cruces to visit relatives." Octavio said this in a straightforward manner. As though he was typing out a story for an article and space was at a premium. I looked away, toward the bus station. I was interested, of course, but I also felt uneasy at being told a personal matter about Evan that he himself had chosen not to divulge. I felt like an unwilling spy intercepting and opening a private letter. The conversation moved on, for which I was thankful.

"What do you know about *el generalisimo*, Vince?"

Octavio was asking me about Pancho Villa. Unlike Penny, who had a degree in American history and was just a few hours short of another in Mexican history from the University of San Francisco, and who knew a great deal about the man and the revolution, I knew very little. Pancho Villa was either a man of legendary greatness or a lout depending on the person you were talking to. He either had sixteen wives or one only, again, depending on the person you were talking to.

"There were those who loved him and those who didn't, I suppose." I said.

"Yes," said Octavio, smiling, "most assuredly. There is passion on both sides. However, the person who wrote the book from which I borrowed was forcefully presenting a viewpoint which is quite common in some circles."

"Which is?"

"Well, in a nutshell, the so-called raid on Columbus, New Mexico, was a triple cross." Octavio ate a few more mouthfuls and then continued.

"In brief, the author, who I tried very hard to track down, wrote that the Americans had discovered that the Germans were interested in establishing an alliance with Villa. In war, of course, there are spies under every other bed. Under the other beds are counter spies. As you know, there was a time during the revolution when the Americans supported Villa against Carranza. Villa was purchasing arms and ammunition from the U.S. right here in El Paso. As a matter of fact what is now the Blue Moon was, back then, a munitions depot." Octavio chewed his food slowly, seemingly to consider what he had just said, or maybe he had perceived the seeds of a story.

Octavio swallowed and continued. "Germany, which was involved in the war in Europe was interested, as a strategic matter, in establishing a base of operations in northern Mexico to thwart the possibility that the U.S. would side with England and France in that war. They reasoned that it would be folly for the Americans to assist allies across the ocean against an enemy who was already situated at their own back door."

What Octavio was saying did not sound all that new to me. It seemed to me that Penny had at one time or another voiced that same general idea. I motioned him to go on.

"Now, Vince, you as a detective should follow this easily." The waitress came over and refilled our coffee cups. Octavio waited until she was gone. "The idea of a flashpoint in 1916 was beneficial to two of the three parties involved. Number one, Germany. If they could entice Villa to attack American soil, it would result in retaliation by the U.S. This would, of course, preoccupy the Americans while Germany could do as it wished in Europe. Number two, America. If the Americans were to have an excuse to send troops into Mexico they could pursue Villa for the purpose of killing him, of course, and thereby remove the possibility that Germany could gain a foothold in northern Mexico."

Octavio wrapped some more bacon inside a tortilla and said, "It is strange, is it not, that two parties seemingly at cross-purposes would have the same objective, no?"

I did not answer but merely sipped my coffee and looked across the street toward the bus station where two young soldiers were walking backwards in front of two young girls who were speaking together and ignoring them. The soldiers parted and the girls walked through still ignoring them. The two soldiers laughed and took off their caps and took turns hitting each other with them.

Octavio continued. "Now, you may not be aware of this, but General Pershing had 7,000 soldiers inside Mexico within six days. Do you have any idea of the logistics involved in mobilizing that many men in that short of a period of time?" I could not answer that question nor did he seem to expect one.

Octavio took a long drink of the hot coffee. It did not seem to bother him. "That leaves the third party, Vince. What would Villa gain from any of this?"

I merely repeated what Penny would say as she covered this same topic. "Nothing."

"Correct. But I am not doing O'Brien's book justice. It is quite complex, full of intrigue and treachery. Some winter night when you are in the mood for chess but lack an opponent let me know. You will find the challenge of chess in O'Brien's story."

I watched as Octavio took his last piece of tortilla and wiped his plate clean. There was nothing left.

"Now, Vince," Octavio took his last sip of coffee, "to his dying day, Villa denied that he had ordered any such attack. There is disagreement, of course. Certainly, but about his demise there is none, seeing as how it was accomplished by about twenty bullet holes." Octavio, with his fingers curved and slightly open, tapped the area over his heart twice. I had the image of a single bullet as it enters the human body, pushing flesh and bone ahead of its deadly path. I thought of what twenty bullets might do.

"Octavio, I see what you are saying but—"

"So," Octavio interrupted, "a plan was set in motion, by the Germans O'Brien alleges, to finance a few soldiers of fortune. That is my term by the way, O'Brien calls them traitors. Now, there were some other men, all paymasters or otherwise involved in the purchase of arms, who had another plan. They decided to steal 70,000 in gold coin and bank notes from Villa's treasury and ride toward Columbus with the others. The number of these traitors was five. These five, with the gold, broke away from the main party about two miles from Columbus. They continued north while the soldiers of fortune rode in to, attacked Columbus, and rode back south leaving a trail. Those men also dumped a few saddlebags of paper incriminating to Villa."

"Now, Vince," Octavio continued, "it so happened that the first initial of the last names of the five, as they were originally listed, spelled the word *basto*. Their last names were: Benavidez, Alcon, Sanchez, Trejo, and Oton."

Now I could see the thread of Octavio's articles. He had written that by the loss of those 70,000 dollars, one of Villa's battalions had suffered a stinging defeat in the battle at the outskirts of Chihuahua City due to the fact that they had not been properly supplied. Villa lost seven hundred and fifty of his best soldiers outright and another two hundred were taken prisoner and hanged from the trees along the main avenue of the city. Octavio had written that someone close to Villa, if not Villa himself, had handpicked another five to track down and kill the traitors. Villa's five had become known as *"carteros"* (postmen) even though one of them, according to Octavio, was a woman.

"Are the names of the *carteros* listed in the book?" I asked.

"No, of course not."

I moved on. "The suit of clubs was the message that the losses at the battle of Chihuahua had been avenged?"

"Correct."

"So, Octavio, in your opinion, the victim last night was a *cartero*?"

"Clearly. You have proved that he killed the others."

"If last night's victim was a *cartero*, who killed him?" I asked.

"Well, Torres said there was no robbery. So it had to be one of the Club, or, since those vendettas can go on from generation to generation, perhaps a son of one of the originals."

There was my opening. I had come here specifically to ask Octavio about Torres' quote but I could not think of a way to do that without casting Torres in a bad light. Octavio was, I had determined, quite perceptive. Even now, he was looking intently into my eyes.

"And the card, what did that mean?" I asked, as I sipped casually of my coffee.

"The ace of clubs?"

"Yes."

Octavio thought for a moment. "A mockery of course. It meant: Your card days are over. You are aced out, man." He lit a cigarette and nodded toward the waitress who moved quickly to our table. Octavio paid her with a crisp, new ten-dollar bill. Octavio gave her a dollar tip, and then he and I sat and made small talk.

I drank my coffee and studied Octavio. There was a strength to him, an extraordinary directness. Something about him, the expressiveness of his face and the way he moved his hands to make a point, reminded me of someone but I could not pinpoint exactly who. An actor, perhaps, or maybe my uncle Santos, who was a union organizer at the docks in San Francisco. Octavio was a man who held his truths, or what he believed to be truths, tightly in both fists. He was not concerned with what he might not know or what others might think of his convictions. I, on the other hand, had many doubts, and what I did not know troubled me very much.

It seemed to me that Octavio and I were in the same boat moving down the same stream, but where he saw fish I saw only shadows. I wondered which one of us was correct.

— 11 —

"**E**thnocentrism." Said Penny, as we lunched on chicken soup and quesadillas at a restaurant not far from the high school.

"Of course." I smiled, not knowing what that word meant and knowing full well she knew I didn't know.

"What that means, Vin, is that each culture views itself as superior to any other culture. One's own culture is the center of the universe. Each culture assigns to itself every virtue, and every vice to the other."

I had described to Penny my meeting with Octavio and about the book he had mentioned, which, I was surprised to learn, she was familiar with. Penny had told me that in her senior year in college she had made extra money by proofreading and editing student papers. She now told me that one of those papers was based on that book. She said she felt that it had been written by one of Villa's female soldiers. I told her how Octavio had explained events in a very different light from the way we, as Americans, were accustomed to. When Penny spoke of these things she spoke as a scholar, a student of history. There was a difference. Now Penny said, "Vin, we tend to forget that the sun rises all over the world and not just in our own neighborhood."

"I see, still, does that make each one's history correct?" I asked.

"Not only correct but solid as a rock that will stand forever, or," Penny paused as she held a spoonful of soup above the bowl, waiting for it to cool, "until you move to another country." She smiled.

Penny was wearing a navy blue suit with a white silk blouse and a gold scarf around her neck. Her light brown hair fell in perfect waves to her shoulders. She looked very pretty. I wondered how many of her students were in love with her.

"Consider this, Vin. Would it make any sense to you if say, during the American Civil War, General Ulysses Grant were to attack some village in Canada?"

"No."

"And suppose the Canada in this example was a very powerful nation, capable of certain retribution. And General Lee, your enemy, was already at the outskirts of your own capitol. Pray tell, what would you gain from such a foolhardy exercise?"

"I can only pray that you will tell me, Mrs. Quiñones." For this, I received a pinch on the wrist.

"Never mind, you. Is there anything new?"

"No. But I spoke with Benny this morning. He saw the killer. I was hoping that perhaps he could remember some other detail." I told Penny what a good-looking kid he was. And smart.

"And the sister, what is her name again?"

"Rosalinda."

"Ah yes, Rosalinda, did you interview her?" Penny looked straight into my eyes.

"No."

"Why not?" Penny cut a piece of quesadilla with knife and fork.

"I don't know. I saw her. But it did not seem the right time to ask her any more questions."

Penny looked up at me. She stopped eating.

"Is she pretty?"

It has been my experience that it is better to answer such questions from one woman about another woman truthfully. If you lie, and they usually know when you are lying, it can go very bad for you. You are not only lying but you are also hiding something. Their imagination will take care of the rest.

"Yes." I said, for which I received a second pinch harder than the first.

"Pretty, yes," I repeated, "but not beautiful like you."

"You." She said, and smiled. There was a blush on her cheeks.

For a moment, I once again had an image of Rosalinda. She was walking down the stairs slowly, smiling at me. I looked across the table at Penny. I reached over and touched her hand.

We ate in silence for a while and when we were finished Penny said, "Vin, there are some errands I need to run after school but the mechanic says that he won't have my car ready until tomorrow. And, we need groceries. Later on, Josie's coming over to go over some new tests. There is no school tomorrow but Josie and I have to do a presentation at the teacher's conference in the afternoon."

"Okay." I said, "Why don't you drop me off at the station and take my car from there. I can catch a ride home later on, or borrow a car from the carpool." As I was saying that, the door flew open and in blew the cold and my former partner, Pete Vereda. He walked in and walked directly to our booth.

"Hey Vince." He said, as he removed his hat and greeted Penny. "I'm sorry to interrupt your lunch but they've been calling for you on the radio. Evan wants you to report for a meeting at one o'clock."

"Well, that solves our problem." I said. "Penny needs the car today. I'll just catch a ride with you Pete, if that's okay, partner."

Pete smiled. "Sure Vince, it'll be like old times."

I walked Penny out to my car and then joined Pete at his squad car. We drove off and Pete said, "Have you heard the latest?"

"What's that, Pete?"

"Well, one of our street people said that here about a month ago Torres lost his ass on the horses across the river. Said Torres thought he had a sure thing and had borrowed money to bet with. The horse broke his leg on the first turn. Torres had to take out a second mortgage on his house which he had damn near lost after his private dick fiasco."

I looked at Pete. He seemed happy. "Well, that's too bad Pete. I feel sorry about that." Pete caught the tone in my voice.

"Yeah, you're right, Vince. Poor sonofabitch."

We drove in silence for a while and then Pete spoke again. "You know, Vince, there are not too many guys who like Torres."

"Yes, I know." I said, as a few drops of rain hit the windshield.

Pete went on. "He just talked too much about how he was going to be his own boss and make a truck load of money with his private dick company. He signed his own death warrant with all his talk and when it didn't fly and he had to come back, well, he just looked like shit after that."

"Pete, that must have been rough on him to have to come back under those circumstances."

"Well, shit, Vince, serves him right. In the first place you and I know that the only way to leave the force in good graces is to retire or better yet be killed in the line of duty."

"I guess you're right, Pete." I felt a sinking feeling. Pete shouldn't have said that. It was bad luck to say such things.

Pete took a few deep breaths and then he said, "And another thing, Vince, the next time Torres starts in with that Detective Q shit, I'm gonna deck him."

I looked at Pete. He had been a good partner to me; the older cop looking after the rookie. But there were times when I could not quite figure him out. For one thing he smiled when he was angry, and he was quick to anger but just as quickly cooled back down.

"It doesn't bother me, Pete." I said.

"Well, just so you know how I feel about that, partner."

I thought of the possibility of Pete and Torres getting into it. They were the same age and had both come out of the Southside. They were the same height; lean and hard muscled, along the lines of natural athletes. If Torres could be called tall, dark, and handsome then Pete could be called tall, white, and handsome. It would be a hell of a fight. Pete could take care of himself, and then some. But I had seen Torres in action. It was in a bar across the bridge. A big, heavily tattooed, mean-looking ex-con by the name of Ramón, who Torres had arrested and sent to prison some time before, approached Torres in a dive on Mariscal and wanted to find out how tough he was without a badge and gun. There were six or seven of us standing at the bar. Torres turned as though to walk away and avoid a fight and then he spun around quickly and drove his elbow into the ex-con's face, sending him to the floor. I thought he was knocked out but he jumped up and charged toward Torres. Torres planted three heavy shots to the eye and temple area of the left side of Ramón's face and he went down again. This time he came up with a knife and lunged at Torres who sidestepped him and kicked him in the chest. Ramón fell again and the knife dropped from his hand. Torres grabbed the knife and placed his knee on the ex-con's neck and started slashing at his face. I had no doubt that Torres would have killed him if we hadn't pulled him off.

The thing that got me was that when Torres turned back to the bar he wasn't shaking or flushed or even breathing heavy. He downed a shot of tequila, chased it with a beer, and said. "Does anybody know if the Dodgers won today?"

A light rain had begun to fall. Pete switched on the windshield wipers.

"You know what else I heard, Vince?"

"What's that, Pete?"

"I heard that Torres has been dating that Lucero girl. You know, the one who's in custody."

"Rosalinda?"

"That's her. Seems like a nice girl. Good looking, too. She could do a hell of a lot better than Torres for cryin' out loud, him married and all. What gets me is that even though he is going out with her he still has the nerve to put the make on all the waitresses at the Blue Moon."

"Where did you hear that, Pete?"

"About the waitresses? Hell, Vince..."

"No. I know about the waitresses. About Rosalinda."

"Hell, Vince, everybody knows that."

Pete kept talking but I did not hear much of what he said. The thing had started in my stomach again. I listened to the rub of the wiper blades. I leaned back and closed my eyes. I thought of the veil on the oleanders, I thought of Benny's question to me, and I thought about Rosalinda. I was thinking thoughts that I did not want to think but the more those thoughts swirled around in my head the clearer it became. I opened my eyes and looked at my hands. They felt cold. I placed them close to the heater vent and rubbed them together while Pete talked nonstop. Could it be possible that Rosalinda plus Torres plus gold equaled a bullet in an old man's chest? The knot in my stomach felt like a chunk of ice.

"They say it don't snow in El Paso," Pete was saying almost to himself, "but it can and does, and if it ain't getting ready to snow right now, I will kiss a pimp's ass!"

— 12 —

Jake Bellamy was sitting in Evan's office when I arrived. Each of them had a cup of steaming coffee in hand. I walked over to the coffeepot as Evan and Bellamy laughed at some old joke.

Bellamy had been with the police department for something like thirty five years. Or, forever, according to the younger guys. In Evan's early years he had been Bellamy's junior partner. Bellamy had moved on from homicide detective to the crime lab in 1940. Usually, Bellamy had excellent insights into crimes of murder until he would begin to lose focus and wander off into the details of some homicide decades before at which time Evan would nudge him back to the case at hand. It seemed to me that the allure of old crime was very strong in Bellamy. I had heard that he still reviewed old, dusty cases on a regular basis. Studying every angle again and again, it was said. Hoping for that certain something to click. I thought that perhaps he kept going back to old cases because when those cases had been fresh, he had been young. It sounded strange to say but Bellamy might look at all those old crime scene photographs in a way another man might look at the picture of an old girlfriend. The one that got away. It was said, and I believed, that Bellamy carried a lock of hair from some old victim in his wallet. I had heard all of the old stories about how every homicide detective would, sooner or later, be involved in a case that would stay with him for the rest of his life. Some case that a detective would even dream about and that it could become his obsession, taking on a life of its own somewhere deep in the recesses of his mind. This had hit home with me on the day that I had been asked to go down to the basement and pull an old file for the Chief, who had been asked about it by some reporter looking into old, unsolved cases.

I had gone down into that musty, badly lit place with one of the filers and we had looked all over but had not been able to find it. The filer had said finally said that perhaps Bellamy had it but he was quite hesitant about going over to his office to ask about it. I, not knowing any better, and in the knowledge that the Chief himself had asked me to get it, had gone into Bellamy's office. He was not there, and sure enough on the top of his desk was the file in question. Inside the cover of the file, on one side, there was a summary of all the individuals interviewed. The dates of the interviews ran from 1929 until 1936. Some of the people had been interviewed as many as ten times. On the other side of the folder, there was a stack of photographs turned upside down. I picked them up and turned them over. They showed the street, the front door, each room of the house, and finally the bedroom. I studied that particular photograph and I had never forgotten it. Hanging on a coat rack in one corner of the bedroom was a wedding dress. The victim was a young woman of perhaps twenty. Even in death, she was quite beautiful. It seemed as though she was merely sleeping. She was on the white sheet of a bed on which there were no blankets. She was wearing no clothes and she was slender and fragile looking. She was lying on her side with one leg partially over the edge of the bed. On the floor by the bed were her shoes, side by side, undisturbed. Usually, in homicide photographs there would be much blood but in that case there were only some tiny droplets that curved over the pillow and onto the sheet in an arc away from her long, dark hair. It was as though she did not have much blood to bleed. I had left a note for Bellamy, saying that I was taking the file at the Chief's request. I had no sooner walked into the Chief's office and handed him the file when Bellamy called him about it.

Now, Evan spoke. "I've asked Bellamy here to see if he can help us on this case, Vinny. I've briefed him on what we learned at the crime scene."

Bellamy looked over at me and then back to Evan and said, "Shouldn't we wait for Torres?"

"He called me," said Evan, "says he's got a lead on the case. He's checking out a guy across the river." I remembered Pete's words and the thought flashed through my mind. *More than likely, he is writing out a check for a guy across the river.* Evan waved Bellamy on. Bellamy frowned as though he had entirely too much work to be messing around with the likes of me. He frowned a lot, and talked to himself sometimes as he wandered down a hallway or sat alone at his desk.

"Okay!" Bellamy said loudly as he stood up and walked to the blackboard. He was a short man with a big voice. He was old, late seventies maybe. Not senile, no, not by a long shot, but definitely eccentric.

"What we want to do here…" he looked at me as though he could not remember my name, "…Vincent, is remove as much bullshit as we can to get to the bones of the matter." He picked up a piece of chalk and quickly drew a column of five squares and a column of five circles. He took a puff from his cigarette and continued. "What's happened here is a serial killer got plugged, right? We have established that Benavidez killed the other three. Why? To silence them of course. Then he leaves a stinking card to throw us off. Wants us to think that the cartels are making good on their pledge to avenge whatever it is that Mr. Eighty-Eight says needs avenging."

I was thinking that Bellamy had pronounced the word *carteros* as *cartels* but I did not say anything, and as far as I knew there had been no change in my expression. Bellamy stopped and looked at me as though I had interrupted him.

"What?" He said.

Surprised, I answered. "I didn't say anything, Bellamy."

Bellamy looked at me for a moment and then said, "*Asi, como no, les dicen los carteros.*" He rolled his "r"s perfectly. I thought to myself, this is one funny old guy. Yeah, funny, and he can read minds.

He smiled at me kindly. "Now, here is some of the bullshit I would like to remove, Vincent. According to Mr. Eighty-Eight the avengers were organized in 1917 yet they do not kill anybody until 1950. Think about it, Vincent. Too much time. There are five people looking for five other people." Bellamy waved his hand down the column of squares and up the column of circles. "Thirty some years go by. Nothing happens. Then, suddenly, they are found and bang, bang, bang, three of the five traitors, as Mr. Eighty-Eight calls them, are dead. No robbery. Nothing taken. Hell, you and I both know those poor bastards didn't have a pot to piss in, for crying out loud."

Bellamy walked over to Evan's desk and extinguished his cigarette.

"Okay, Vince?" Bellamy said as he walked back to the blackboard and erased three of the five squares from the bottom up. "Now, last night, bang again." He erased the fourth square.

Bellamy circled the lone remaining square and picked up the pointer. "Is this our man?" Bellamy asked, as he tapped the pointer against the blackboard at the top square. "No. He is already dead. He either died of natural causes or was killed prior to 1950 somewhere else. How do we know this, you ask? Because, if he had been alive and here in our fair city, Benavidez would have killed him also." Bellamy erased the final square.

"Any questions, Vince?"

"You're saying that there was no *cartero* involvement in the previous three—"

Bellamy interrupted me. "I'm saying there was no *cartero* involvement whatsoever. I'm saying that the *carteros* never existed except as they were invented by Mr. Eighty-Eight." Bellamy turned back to the blackboard and put a slash through each circle as is used to differentiate a zero from the letter "O." He stepped back and studied the column of zeroes. I looked at Evan to see his reaction to what Bellamy was saying but he had his head down writing on a notepad.

Bellamy placed one arm under the other and placed his free hand up to his chin. He moved his head slowly, up and down the column. "I would say, gentlemen, now correct me if I'm wrong here, that five times zero is zero." With that, he removed the column of circles with one long swipe of the eraser. The blackboard was clean. Bellamy walked back to his chair and lit another cigarette.

Bellamy looked over at Evan and said, "What was the name of that circus, Evan?"

Evan looked up, thought for a second, and said. "Benton Brothers."

"Right." Looking at me, Bellamy began talking. "Well, Evan and I walk into the big tent at six in the morning and see the young lady at the foot of the ladder which led up to the tight rope. She is dead. Looks like she fell those forty feet. She's wearing her blue and gold costume, all sparkly and everything." Bellamy stopped and took a long drag from his cigarette. I looked at Evan but his attention was on Bellamy.

"The high wire act was billed as Sky High Ty and…what was her name, Evan?"

"Cloud Maid." Said Evan.

"Yes," continued Bellamy, "Sky High Ty and his daring assistant, the beautiful Cloud Maid."

I was not interested in some old case. I had much too much to think about regarding the case at hand. I had a lot of sorting and sifting to do. But Bellamy was looking straight at me and I was compelled to listen.

"Did you ever see them perform, Evan?" Bellamy asked this of Evan even though he was looking at me.

"No, I never had the pleasure, Jake."

"Well, I did. Sky High would walk out on the rope and Cloud Maid would walk out from the other side. He would lower his balancing pole and she would step up on it and onto his shoulders and then sort of slide down his back. He would turn on the wire while switching hands on the pole and then they would do it again. It was pretty amazing." Bellamy paused, as though waiting for me to say something. All I could think to say was, "Sounds amazing, Bellamy." I looked at Evan. His look to me said, if you want to stop him you had better stop him now. But by that time, Bellamy was already going.

"Well now, the story was that the beautiful Cloud Maid had made a mistake at that night's performance and had stayed late practicing her moves, which sounded strange since the spotlight move was the one I just described. That is, if she needed to practice she would need a partner. That and the fact that she had fallen directly beneath the small platform which extended maybe eighteen inches from the top of the ladder. The rope near the ladders at both ends was quite thick and only got thinner as it stretched out over the net. In other words she had not yet gotten to the thin part of the rope and therefore over the net when she had fallen." Bellamy reached into his pocket for his pack of cigarettes, noticed he had one lit in the ashtray, picked it up and took a puff.

"Now, the beautiful Cloud Maid does not look so pretty. I mean, besides being dead and lying there in the sawdust and all that. Nope, not pretty at all. Her hair is quite mussed up and her lipstick looks like something a little girl who is playing grown up might apply. There is also a tiny feather stuck between her left earlobe and the skin beneath it. I kneeled down and noticed that she had some dried blood and what looked like skin underneath her fingernails. I am thinking murder and if it is murder then I am thinking that Sky High, who is her husband, needs to be interviewed. Evan here, is kneeling right beside me and we both get the same thought at the same time because we say, in unison, 'She was suffocated.' So, I send Evan over to Sky-High's trailer and he comes back in about two minutes with Sky High in cuffs and says 'tell Detective Bellamy what you told me'. Sky High confesses without ever looking down at the body. Says the beautiful Cloud Maid had a lover and he put a pillow over her head until she stopped scratching and then carried her up the ladder and dropped her. Said he didn't believe in divorce." Pausing only long enough to take a puff of his cigarette, Bellamy went on. "Remember old lady Tidlane, who lived out by the Fort somewhere?"

Evan spoke quickly, "How could I forget, Jake? That was excellent detective work on your part."

"Well, it was staring us in the face, if you know what I mean, Evan." Bellamy let out a hearty laugh. Evan smiled at him and said, "Jake, what can you tell us about last night's case?"

Bellamy stopped laughing and said, "Let me think a bit, Evan." He looked up at the blackboard and seemed to study it. It was blank, of course, since he had wiped it clean moments before. His eyes moved back and forth, as though he was reading some words written there.

"Okay." Bellamy said, and stepped up to the blackboard again. "You say robbery's the motive, Evan?"

"That's my feeling, Jake. I believe that that trunk held quite a bit of gold coin."

"The linoleum is replaced when?" Bellamy asked.

I spoke up. "Benny said last month."

"Who's Benny?"

"The boy, Rosalinda's little brother, the eye witness." I responded.

"Did he know the trunk was there?"

"No." I said. "Benny told me that when he got home from school, the linoleum had already been replaced by his uncle and, you know, Vesuvio, from across the bridge."

"Vesuvio? That reminds me, I've got some stuff ..." Bellamy did not finish. Instead, he took out a piece of crumpled paper from his vest pocket and tried to write something on the paper with the piece of chalk. He laughed, and then took out a pencil from another pocket and made a note, which he studied for a few moments. He put pencil and paper back into his pocket and then picked up the chalk again and drew a large triangle on the blackboard.

"Do you think Miss Lucero knew the trunk was there?" He asked me.

"Yes, Benny said she was home on the day the linoleum was replaced."

"That was on a Thursday?"

"Yes." I said. "He had a routine, store closed every Thursday around noon."

Bellamy wrote the victim's name outside one of the points of the triangle. Then he wrote Rosalinda's name outside another point and Vesuvio's outside the third point.

Bellamy mused. "Hmmm, I think that an old man with a trunk full of gold would want to look at it once in a while. Dip his hands into the gold, let it run through his fingers. You know, like Silas Marner..."

Evan spoke. "Jake, we believe that the murder was committed because the killer knew the victim would know who robbed him."

Bellamy spoke to Evan. "So, the arrow that points to Miss Lucero also points away from her?"

"Yes. If she was going to rob him why wait around? Or, why kill him at all? Simply take the money one Thursday and leave. She and the boy could have been on the train to Guadalajara that very afternoon. He would have never found her."

I spoke up. "And beyond that, Benny heard the killer's voice. It was not her. It was a man."

Bellamy turned back to the blackboard and studied it for a moment. He erased Vesuvio's name. Then he drew a line through Rosalinda's name. He picked up the pointer and placed it by Rosalinda's crossed out name. He studied the blackboard for what seemed a very long time. Finally, he spoke.

"Well then, gentlemen, I would say that the probability is very high that our young Miss Lucero has a lover." As Bellamy said those words, he slammed the pointer hard against the blackboard.

Bellamy came back and sat down. He seemed tired. He and Evan lit cigarettes. Outside, the light was fading fast. The room was silent except for the windblown rain hitting the window behind Evan's desk. It sounded like sleet. I reached up to loosen my tie and noticed that my hands were shaking.

Bellamy finished his cigarette and stood up to leave. Evan thanked him as he walked out while I sat and looked at the triangle and Rosalinda's crossed out name. Evan made a few more notes in his notepad and then said, "I don't believe you've ever met my mother have you, Vinny?"

"No, Evan."

"Do you have any plans for tonight?"

"No. Penny will be out running errands and then she and Josie are going to work on devising tests, I think. No plans."

"Good. Come with me. I would like you to meet the woman who saved my life."

13

We drove by Evan's apartment on Montana Street first. He left the motor running and the heater on for me as he went up to check his mail and make a telephone call. I sat in the car and watched the people hurrying by. A young woman with a small boy at her side walked by. She was leaning over him with her umbrella to shield him from the rain.

Bellamy's presentation was on my mind. He had removed much from the broadness of the investigation. Like some old bloodhound, he would not chase just any random scent. No. Bellamy had sliced everything away but bare bone. But why had Evan remained silent when Bellamy said that there were no *carteros*? Was it merely a respectful silence? Evan had said that Octavio was right, in general. How general was general? I wondered.

"Miss Lucero has a lover!" Bellamy's words had coincided with the whack of the pointer that sounded like the crack of a pistol shot. It had had a strange effect on me. The muscles in my throat had closed, hard.

It had been one thing for me to suspect that Rosalinda had a lover, and that her lover was Torres, and that between them they had stolen Benavidez' gold. That hypothesis was mine. It existed in my mind only, as far as I knew. I could embrace my suspicions or discard them at will since they were my own. But to have a part of my suspicions spoken out loud with such emphasis and forcefulness had startled me. I had not wanted to admit it because I could not explain it. Bellamy's words had frightened me. I put the idea aside when Evan returned and we drove back towards downtown and turned north on Stanton. We drove on Stanton and then turned on Blanchard and followed it to a curving side street to an area of the city I was not familiar with.

I had heard that back in the 1890's El Paso's upper class had built their mansions in that area. An enclave of the rich. They were mostly two-story red brick colonial structures with white pillars. Those homes were still well maintained but the new rich, that is, the sons and daughters of those original builders had moved out to the foothills and built large, sprawling ranch homes. Now, the mansions in that area were inhabited mostly by the elderly.

It was at the side of one of those residences that Evan parked his car. We ascended some wide steps and as we crossed the portico the wide front door opened. A maid dressed in black and white smiled broadly at Evan.

"Good evening, Mercedes, is mother still up?"

"Yes, Don Estevan, I shall inform her that you are here." She looked at me and smiled.

"Mercedes, this is my partner, Detective Vincent Quiñones."

"With much pleasure" said Mercedes as she curtsied and took our hats and coats.

Evan led me down a wide hallway and then we turned to the right into a large room. There was a fire burning in a large flagstone fireplace from which came the aroma of juniper. A chandelier illuminated several oil paintings on the walls. I recognized the styles of Orozco and Velasquez but I did not know if they were originals or reproductions. I had seen the works of those two painters on display at the Museum of Art in San Francisco.

On another wall, and in a different style, was the painting of a young woman. She had dark flowing hair, which came down past her shoulders. The young woman was turned slightly to her left and looking up at something out of the picture. Behind her were long fields of green. She was quite beautiful and resembled none other than the actress Susan Hayward. I was wondering if it was indeed the actress when Evan said: "That is my wife, Sonia. Mother painted her."

I turned to speak to Evan but he was already hurrying up the curved stairway to the second floor. He called back. "Please have a seat, Vinny. I'll be back down shortly."

I moved toward the fireplace and sat on a long plush sofa. I was studying the dance of the flames when out of the corner of my eye I saw a small person enter the room. She was smiling and moving toward me. She had silver hair and wore a light gray shawl over a blue blouse and blue slacks. She was the tiniest woman I had ever seen. Elfin, I suppose, would be the word. She was a perfectly proportioned miniature woman.

"Detective Quiñones, I gather." She said with the voice of a full-sized woman.

I stood up as she approached. She offered me a small hand and I, without a second thought, as though I had done this all my life, bent down and kissed it.

"A pleasure to meet you, Mrs. Morrow." I said as I looked into the brightest blue eyes I had ever seen.

She laughed a full-bodied laugh. "Please, call me Helen." And then, in perfect Spanish, she said: "*Bienvenido. Nuestra casa es su casa.*"

I thanked her as we sat together on the sofa. At that moment, Evan appeared at the top of the stairs and Mercedes entered the living room. They both spoke at the same time. Evan said, "I see you two have met." while Mercedes said, "Can I get the gentlemen anything, Doña Elena?"

Evan's mother laughed and answered, "Yes, Evan, and yes, Mercedes." Then, directing her words to Mercedes she said: "Please bring us some red wine, dear."

Evan came down the stairs. He had removed his suit jacket and tie and was wearing a black cardigan sweater over his white shirt.

"Evan," said his mother, "the man last night, he was the person from Santa Rosa?"

"Yes, mother."

Evan's mother looked at him for a long moment. It seemed to me that there was pain in her eyes. "You know I am deeply sorry."

"Yes. Thank you, mother."

Mercedes entered the room. She had a graceful walk. She was carrying a tray with three glasses of wine. One was a small, narrow glass; the other two were full-size. Evan's mother was speaking.

"I am afraid that we did not have anything special for dinner, gentlemen, but perhaps if Mercedes would be so kind."

From the tray, Mercedes handed us each our glass of wine. "Yes, Doña Elena. Would the gentlemen care for a sandwich, perhaps?"

Evan answered. "Please, Mercedes. Sandwiches would be fine. Thank you." Mercedes smiled at Evan as she bowed slightly and left the room.

Evan and his mother and I drank our wine and spoke together. The conversation was not about crime but about the cold weather and other things. I told Evan's mother that I was from San Francisco as was my wife, and that although we had never met there we did have some acquaintances in common.

"What a remarkable coincidence" she said, "that fate should cause each of you to travel a thousand miles to meet here when you could have just as easily bumped into each other on a sidewalk there." She took a small sip of wine, and then she said, "Life is so interesting, so full of sweetness and, sad to say, heartbreak."

On our way to the kitchen, we passed through a long room with many windows. There were several paintings, in various stages, on easels all along the inside wall. I gathered that Mrs. Morrow was not only a painter but beyond that an artist. One painting, in particular, struck me. It showed a bronze-skinned young girl, blond, nude, with her back to the artist, sitting cross-legged on a beach. The girl was facing a large, gray, oblong boulder that jutted out of the sand. Beyond the boulder, there was a translucent blue-green wave about to break upon the shore. In a way that I could neither understand nor explain, the shadow of the boulder seemed to have left impressions on the sand in the manner of a receding wave.

We walked into a large kitchen and sat at a small table next to a window. Mercedes served us grilled ham and cheese sandwiches with lettuce and tomato on thick slices of toasted French bread. The sandwiches had been cut in half and alongside them were large black olives. Next to the plates Mercedes placed a bowl of steaming potato soup and refilled our wineglasses. She served Evan's mother a small piece of Mexican pastry and hot cocoa.

The table was up against a long window. Evan and I sat facing each other. He had not been quite himself last night but now he was relaxed and smiled often at his mother who was sitting to my right, facing the window. The years seemed to drop away from Evan's face. Outside of this place, this house, he was one of those rare individuals who commanded respect and admiration both on the street and in high places. But here he was merely a mother's son sitting at her table. Sometimes, as we ate, I looked at Mrs. Morrow's reflection in the window. There was something fairy-like about her. Her image enchanted me, as did her lilting voice and measured words.

14

After we were finished eating and had said goodnight to Evan's mother, he and I walked up the stairs to what I assumed was his study. There was a fire burning in a fireplace there also. In one corner, there was a roll top desk with a floor lamp beside it. At the outer wall was a large, many-paned window, which went from the floor to the ceiling. Another wall was filled with books. In the middle of the room were two plush, brown leather chairs facing the fireplace. Between the chairs, there was a small round table on which sat a pitcher of ice and water, two tall glasses, and a decanter of liquor.

Above the mantle of the fireplace was a framed, glass-covered color photograph. That is, I believed it was a photograph until I looked closely. It was actually a masterfully rendered watercolor painting of a town in the mountains. I knew that it had to be the town Evan and his mother had mentioned: Santa Rosa.

The town was nestled in mountains. The mountain to the right seemed to be of sheer rock, which was a pinkish gold in color, and the one to the left was wooded. Behind the town, and towering above the other two mountains, was a mesa that was more heavily wooded and on whose cliffs was the same pinkish gold. Above the mesa, storm clouds were beginning to show but above that was a deep-blue sky. The sun was shining directly on the town. A winding road led up to the town, appearing and disappearing as it wound its way up the mountain.

In what appeared to be the main street of the town there were several two and three-story buildings. There were a few houses below the buildings but the main concentration of houses rose above the town in tiers, one above the other, packed tight, with paths and long rising steps which seemed to join each ascending tier.

"Remarkable work is it not, Vinny?"

"Yes. This is Santa Rosa?"

"Yes. Mother painted it for me shortly after she adopted me. It was the site of one of the richest copper mines in the country. Way back it was gold, then the gold gave way to copper."

Evan poured each of us a drink. Looking out of the window to the streetlight on the corner, I could see that it had begun to snow.

Drink in hand, Evan walked over to the window and looked out. After a moment, he said, "It would snow in Santa Rosa. Quite heavy at times." He came back and sat in the other chair.

"*Salud.*" Evan said, as he raised his glass to mine.

"*Salud.*" I said. The scotch was cold and smooth going down and then warm as it hit my stomach.

Evan pointed to the painting and began speaking softly. "Between that mountain and the mesa there was a deep, narrow canyon. A spring issued from a thin crack in the canyon wall down at the bottom. The water was always cold, even in summer; no doubt it came from melted snow. I would refill my homemade canteen there, which was a whiskey pint bottle wrapped in canvas." Evan smiled and thought for a moment and then continued. "The trickling spring formed a pool, and in the damp sand around the pool you could see the tracks of bear, deer, mountain lion, and wolf. There was a long bench-like groove in the rock and it was there that

I would rest on my way back home from my wood gathering trips. One day I had found an interesting piece of oak root, which was in the shape of a coiled snake about to strike. I thought that with just a bit of whittling I could form the head and fangs and maybe sell it to Don Felipe who owned a store where he sold herbs and other curios. I took out my pocketknife and was about to begin whittling when I heard a rustling along one of the game paths that led to the pool. A young wolf, a pup really, appeared and looked at me. He was no more than twenty feet away. Right behind the wolf appeared a doe. They came to the pool and drank, side by side, until they were full and then they moved away and disappeared back up into the bushy path. You are aware, Vinny, that it is said that the wolf is the mortal enemy of the deer?"

I nodded, and Evan continued. "I don't know if seeing what I had just seen or the fact that I had walked a long way caused me to feel quite peaceful and drowsy but that is how I felt. I leaned back and as I was looking up at the opposite canyon wall a few doves landed on a shrub pine, which grew out of a ledge. A breeze ran through the canyon. I closed my eyes and listened to the cooing of the doves. I suppose I drifted off for just a moment and when I opened my eyes, I saw a dark figure moving along the sandy canyon bottom headed straight toward me. It was quite low to the ground. I thought that it was a javelina at first but it did not kick up any dust. Then I realized that it was a shadow. It stopped right at my feet. I looked up and directly above me, not more than forty feet in the air was a golden hawk. He hovered there as though suspended in air. His wings were motionless. Then, straight as an arrow, he dove toward the shrub pine. The doves sprang up, trying to escape, but the hawk, using his wings, beat two of the doves back, containing them. In an instant he clutched one in each claw. And then he began to rise straight up, again without moving his wings although

I suppose he was tilting them in such a way as to use an air current. He rose straight up as though drawn on a string and then passed up and over the canyon wall and out of my sight." Evan looked at me.

I said, "That is an interesting story, Evan." He looked out through the window and then back at me. "Well," he sighed, "it was an interesting place, Vinny." Evan smiled.

Evan offered me a cigarette, lit mine and then lit his. "The victim last night. His real name was Benavidez. I knew him in Santa Rosa. Rather, when I was a boy, he was posing as a woman by the name of Doña Fortuna."

Evan had said this last night but all of his conversation had taken me by surprise. I hadn't known what to ask. Even now all I could say was, "A woman?"

"Yes, an old woman who only went out at night. All the kids were afraid of her. Some said she was *"La Llorona."* Evan smiled. "You are familiar with that legend, Vinny?"

I was. It was ancient folklore. The old woman who would never die. The mother who in some way had caused the death of her children and was condemned to walk the earth forever. On black nights she came. Weeping, wailing, howling for her lost children. And stealing bad children whenever she could get them. Yes, there was many a child who had gone to bed after misbehaving and fear the darkness and the howling of the wind for it might be the ugly, wrinkled, deathless one coming to take them from their beds. In the morning they would laugh at her, of course, and misbehave again.

"I believe that she killed my father." Evan took a drink and tapped the ash from his cigarette into a large copper ashtray, which had been cast in the shape of the outline of the state of Arizona.

Evan continued. "I do not believe that my father, may he rest in peace, was a *cartero*. He was from the town of Parral, however, and Doña Fortuna, who was definitely a *basto*, must have suspected that he was a *cartero* and acted on that suspicion. My father was stabbed to death one night on his way home from the mine."

I spoke. "I am sorry, Evan." Evan was looking at the painting of Santa Rosa. I spoke again. "So, there were indeed *bastos* and *carteros?*"

"Most definitely, Vinny. I saw the proof first hand."

Evan poured us another drink. I looked out at the falling snow and then back at the flames in the fireplace.

"Three weeks after my father was murdered, my mother took ill. She went to bed and could not get up again. She died two weeks later. I was ten years old."

"My God, Evan."

"My Aunt Belen, my mother's sister, took me in. It was hard. She had eight kids of her own. To help out, I would go up into the mountains and gather firewood after school to sell. I also worked at Don Jose's barbershop, cleaning up and shining shoes. Whatever money I earned I gave to my aunt."

Evan pointed to the painting and said, "There is another town at the bottom of those mountains. It is called Orenville. The railroad ended there. Sometimes, traveling salesmen would come to Orenville and then walk up that road to Santa Rosa. If I saw one coming up I would run down and offer to help him with his suitcases. There was a mule train that ran between the two towns but I never saw a salesman take it. They always walked. Usually, they would give me a nickel."

"One day, about a year after the death of my parents, I saw such a salesman come limping up the road. He was a large, Anglo-looking man from Mexico. His name was Jacob Bingham. He told me later that his father had been Mormon and his mother Mexican. He sold bibles and other religious articles. That is, that was his cover, he was actually a *cartero.*"

Evan took a long drink from his glass, as did I.

"He had two suitcases. A large one and a smaller one plus a leather bag slung over his shoulder. I reached for the large suitcase but he handed me the smaller one. As we walked up the winding road he asked me my name. I said, Estevan Valenzuela."

"That is your birth name, Evan?" I asked.

"Yes. I believe I had a mouthful of food when mother asked me my name. I suppose that I did not pronounce it fully. She heard 'Evan' and I let it go."

Evan poured us another drink and then continued. "Jacob said, 'Valenzuela, you say? What is your father's name?' Manuel, I said.

"He asked me if there were any other Valenzuelas in the town of Santa Rosa. No, just me, my father and mother are both dead, I answered. By this time, Jacob and I were walking along the crowded main street. He smiled at everyone."

Evan pointed to the painting and said, "Jacob took a room at the Hotel St. Rose, which is the third building to the left of that red building there." I looked up at the picture and found the hotel.

"We became friends. I enjoyed being with him. He taught me how to play chess. It began to dawn on me that this man was there to find my father's killer. It was the way he asked me about the death; the day, the time of day, had he been robbed, did anyone have any idea who may have done it. He was very interested in it and I did not mind answering his questions. The matter had been investigated but there were no witnesses and no suspect had ever been named. It was just one of those things."

Evan went on. "Jacob Bingham was born and raised a Mormon in a Mormon colony in Chihuahua. At the age of six his family was caught in a crossfire between two factions. Jacob was the only survivor and he was taken in by Villa's army. At the battle of Aguascalientes, Jacob's horse was shot from under him and it landed on Jacob's left leg, smashing it badly. He walked with a pronounced limp."

Evan poured us another drink. "Jacob asked me if I knew a man by the name of Benavidez, and gave me a description of him including the fact that he had a birthmark on the back of his neck in the shape of a triangle and that the little finger on his left hand was missing."

I asked. "The long hair of Doña Fortuna would have covered the birthmark?"

"Exactly, plus the fact that he was asking about a man and not a woman."

"And you never saw Doña Fortuna during the day, Evan?"

"I do not recall that I ever did. Occasionally, she would walk down the trail from her house to the grocery store after sundown. I always made it a point to steer clear of her. She painted her face white with very red lips. She wore a sweet, overpowering perfume." Evan paused, remembering, it seemed to me.

"One evening, in November, after Jacob had been there about a month, a note was placed in my shoeshine box at the barber shop. There had been snow flurries on and off all afternoon. It was a little after 7:00 in the evening when Don Jose looked out the window and said, 'I believe a storm is coming. I am going to close early. Why don't you finish up and go on home?'

"I walked back to the storage room to put away my push broom and dustpan. As I opened the drawer that held my shoe shining supplies, I saw the envelope. Written on the outside of the envelope were the words, 'Deliver to Jacob Bingham'.

"I had no idea how that envelope had gotten there but whoever had done that had meant for me to find it, of course. I quickly stuffed it in my back pocket and came back toward Don Jose and asked him if anyone had maybe borrowed some of my supplies. He was sitting on his barber's chair reading a Mexican newspaper. He peered up over the paper and said, 'No, no one has borrowed any of your things.' He said again, 'You better run along now, before the storm.'

"Yes, I said, I'll just use the restroom and be on my way. Of course, I went into the restroom and read the note. It was written in Spanish. In essence what it said was: Señor Bingham, I know the identity of the person you are seeking. It would be very dangerous for me to be seen with you. Please meet me at the end of the road above the town by the black rock at 8:00 o'clock tonight. Take care that no one follows you.

"I walked out of the barbershop knowing full well that Don Jose must have placed the letter in my shoeshine box. He was looking at me as I walked out so I walked up the street under the streetlights as I normally would if I was heading towards the hotel.

"As soon as I had gone around the curve, I cut back beneath and back around, and, staying in the shadows, I positioned myself in the dark entryway of a store opposite the barbershop. Sure enough, a minute later, Doña Fortuna appeared and walked by the barbershop, looking in. By the light of the shop, I saw her raise her head slightly the way people do when asking a silent question. Don Jose answered her with two nods. Doña Fortuna passed on and then crossed the street and started walking back toward where I was pressed into the shadows. It was cold and I was quite afraid. I held my breath. She did not see me. I smelled her sickly sweet perfume as she went by.

"After she went around the curve I waited a minute or so and then, sticking to the shadows, made my way to the hotel. I walked up the stairs to the second floor and knocked on Jacob's room door. I handed him the envelope and he removed the letter and read it."

Evan poured us another drink, this one with only a splash of water. He stood up and placed more wood on the fire. I looked up at him. He seemed very far away. Afraid that he would stop now, I said, "It is a very interesting story, Evan." He looked into the flames for a few moments and then came back and sat down.

"Jacob walked over to the closed curtains and opened and shut them twice. The metal rings on the metal curtain rod made a scraping sound. For a moment I thought that he was signaling someone outside, perhaps someone in the town below. But then, I heard a door slam on the floor above us and shortly thereafter there was a knock on the door. By this time Jacob was standing by the door and opened it slightly. He whispered something that I could not make out and handed the letter to whoever was at the door. I heard another whisper and then the door was closed.

"Jacob walked back to a small desk beside his bed, opened the drawer and removed a deck of cards. With one quick movement, he fanned the cards out in a half circle. He removed the queen of clubs and, face up, folded the four corners down so that it resembled a small table and placed it on the desk. He pulled out a suitcase from underneath his bed and took out a pistol, which he placed next to the folded card."

I spoke quickly. "Evan, last night, when you said that Mr. Ochoa was right in general, is that what you meant?"

"Yes. At the time of the other murders, I was not convinced that they were the work of the *carteros* because of the way the cards were folded. I considered it a ruse."

A thought flashed through my mind but it was too quick for me to catch. I looked at my watch. It was 10 o'clock. Twenty-four hours had passed since last night's homicide. I watched Evan pour us another drink. I did not want to think about last night. Not yet, at any rate.

"Jacob said to me, he had not spoken since greeting me when I had arrived, 'your father and I fought side by side in the revolution. He was a good man. He carried me off the battlefield at Aguascalientes when my horse fell on my leg. The man who killed him mistook him for someone else but by killing him exposed himself as the despicable traitor that he is.' He looked at me for a long while. 'Son, I must do this tonight and having done it I must flee. You will not see me again.'

"Jacob picked up the card and put it inside his coat pocket. He placed the pistol inside his belt. He put on his hat and coat and knelt down to embrace me. He stood up and shook my hand and told me to go home."

Evan stood up and tended the fire. It crackled as he pushed the poker into the flaming coals. He added another piece of wood to it and came back and sat down.

"I did not go home. I took the straight path instead of the winding road. What we called 'the black rock' was a huge, flat topped, solid rock formation, which jutted out of the mountain at the end of the road. Just before the rock began, there was a lone, large pine tree. The rock was very hard; I do not know what it is called. On the cliff side of the rock, someone had chiseled out a narrow path and made an exploratory tunnel into it. It was a shallow cave. I waited there.

"After a few minutes I heard footsteps and I came out of the cave and back around on the path. Behind me lay a chasm a hundred and fifty feet deep. I peeked up over the rock. In the light of a half-moon I saw Jacob. A few moments later I saw Doña Fortuna come up over the last rise in the road.

"Jacob said, 'You have some information for me, Señora?' "

I heard her say 'yes, it is written on this paper.' She approached Jacob with a piece of paper in her extended hand. Jacob reached for the paper. I saw the flash of the knife in the moonlight. Doña Fortuna's other hand moved very quickly in an upward motion.

"Jacob did not make a sound. He dropped to his knees still holding Doña Fortuna's hand. She withdrew the knife and plunged it again. Jacob began to rise and then staggered back and fell over the edge. Doña Fortuna stepped to the edge and giggled. My heart was at my throat." Evan stopped talking and looked into the flames of the fireplace. A vision of what Evan was saying to me came into my mind with the clarity of a motion picture.

Evan cleared his throat. He said something under his breath and then spoke again out loud. "Suddenly, a figure materialized from behind the big tree. A woman dressed in black. I could see her face clearly. I knew everyone in that town but this woman I had never seen before. Very quickly, she moved toward Doña Fortuna. Doña Fortuna must have heard the footsteps. She was halfway turned around when the woman pushed her mightily over the edge. A long scream of horror came from Doña Fortuna as she fell those hundred and fifty feet.

"The woman looked down. She was young, and tall. I will never forget the look on her face, nor can I describe it. She opened her arms wide as though she was going to jump but she did not. A long, low sob came from deep within her, and then she turned and ran back down the road.

"I began to shake with such force that I had no control over my body. I thought I was going to freeze to death, or die of fear. I didn't know which. I was sick. Then, I too, ran back down the road."

Evan stood up and walked to the window. I looked back into the flames of the fireplace and waited. Once again I saw the image of Evan as a young boy, witnessing the murder of his friend.

Evan returned to his chair. "In the morning they found the bodies, as I knew they would, since at the bottom of the chasm was the main trail that we all used on our wood gathering trips.

"They brought both bodies out on litters and took them to the infirmary to do autopsies. When they removed Doña Fortuna's clothes they saw that she was a man and he came to. Benavidez was alive although half-frozen. Apparently he had landed on some bushes which had broken his fall.

"The sheriff placed him under arrest for murder and threw him in the jail, which was actually a shallow, L-shaped cave with bars. All the boys went by to taunt him. They would try to throw rocks at him through the bars.

"The sheriff was pretty disgusted at seeing a man with long hair so he sent Don Jose to cut it. And, for some reason, Benavidez could not be tried for murder there in Santa Rosa. That had to be done in Tucson. That afternoon Don Jose closed his shop, and that night I saw him carrying some things down from Benavidez' house on a mule.

"The sheriff sent a deputy to transport Benavidez by train to Tucson. Word came back the next day that Benavidez had escaped and jumped off of the train. A posse was sent out but he was not found. The next morning Don Jose was gone also.

"I went to Jacob's funeral. The cemetery was on a small hill opposite my aunt's house. I thought that the woman who loved him would be there but she wasn't. That night however, from my window, I saw a figure dressed in white moving among the graves. The next morning before sunrise I left a note for Aunt Belen and took off. I headed for Tucson. I reasoned that if they were taking Benavidez there under arrest for murder, he would not go that way on his own.

- 95-

"Not walking along the railroad track itself, but always keeping it in sight, I followed it to Tucson. It took me a week, mostly because several times I would just lie down and wait for death to take me. But then I wouldn't die and I would get up and start walking again.

"It was during one of those times that I had a very vivid dream. I saw a beautiful angel. She was smiling down on me and speaking but I could not understand her words. The next day I saw that angel. It was mother."

Evan did not speak for a long while. We both sat there and looked at the fire. The level of the scotch in the decanter was down low. I glanced at my watch. It was 11:45.

Evan came back from wherever his thoughts had carried him. "Now, Vinny, all of this leads us to last night's homicide. On the surface we have a Club killing, right? Benavidez fits the bill. He is the right age, and Mexican, and the money is left in the cash register. The sequence of the cards is correct, as far as the newspapers are concerned, that is, four, three, two, and one. So the killer walks in, speaks a few words, shoots Benavidez and leaves the card. Now, I am not ready to rule out the possibility that it was a woman. But here is my major question, Vinny. Did the killer know that Benavidez was the killer of the other three? And, if he or she did have this knowledge, then that would be something that a force of over one hundred police officers, not to mention a dozen or so undercover people, could never find out. And I would say that we should spare no expense in hiring this individual as a detective." Evan's words struck me as very funny and I laughed a little too loudly. Evan looked at me. Apparently he had not meant the words to be funny but then catching my gusto he did chuckle. "Right, Vinny?"

"Right, Evan."

"So, Vinny, if we proceed on the assumption that the killer did know, we are drawn into a strange case, and if we assume that he or she did not know, we are drawn into a case that is stranger still." Evan stopped talking again and looked into the fire. His face grew quite pensive and after a few moments his eyes closed.

"Evan, I think I better go on home." I said, softly.

Evan opened his eyes but without turning toward me said, "Take my car, Vince, I'll have Mercedes drive me to the station in the morning."

I drove home over the pure whiteness of undisturbed snow.

—— 15 ——

When I got home Penny and Josie were out in the front yard throwing snowballs at each other. The snowballs were only slightly larger than golf balls and seemed to break up before they got very far. When I stepped out of the car they joined forces in attacking a common target but they didn't hit me a single time as I walked nonchalantly toward the steps to the front porch.

"Goodnight, Josefina." I called out to Josie, which was the name she hated to be called.

"Oh yeah?" She huffed. Her aim improved slightly and I felt a snowball hit the back of my shoe. I was tempted to call Penny by her real name also. She knew what I was thinking, however, and said, "Don't you dare!"

I stood on the porch and watched as Josie got into her car and rolled down her window. She started giggling and so did Penny. They couldn't stop. I wondered how much wine they had imbibed. That was their favorite word when they drank wine. They used it quite a bit. Sometimes I thought that the word had a secret meaning for them. Like a private joke. Finally, they stopped giggling and Josie drove off.

I thought I heard the telephone but when I stepped inside it had stopped ringing. I walked back out to the kitchen and sat at the kitchen table. Penny came in and stood at the doorway, leaning on the side, with one hand on her hip, and said, "So, what do you have to say for yourself, sailor?" She sounded exactly like Lauren Bacall. I didn't know if she was trying to imitate her or if it was the wine.

I laughed. "Is there any wine left in the city of El Paso?"

"Nope, we imbibed it all." Penny said, and started giggling again. She sashayed over to the table with one hand on her hip and sat down opposite me. We each got a cigarette from a pack that Josie had left behind.

Penny looked into my eyes. "You seem serious, Vin. Anything wrong?"

I told Penny about my meeting with Bellamy and Evan, and about Mrs. Morrow and the house and the paintings.

"Evan's mother has a maid?" Penny asked.

"Well, she does wear a uniform, Penny, but I gathered that she was more of a companion or even a friend."

I began to tell Penny Evan's story. "Jacob Bingham?" She interrupted.

"Yes."

"Could that be the 'J.B.' of the book?"

"What?"

"The book, don't you remember that Octavio said that it was dedicated to 'J.B.'"

I had not thought of that but I told Penny I supposed it could be. I continued with the story.

Penny said. "So, the dead man from last night was the person who murdered Evan's father back in Santa Rosa?"

"Yes."

"And the man from Mexico was sent to investigate?"

"Yes, Penny."

"And this Jacob Bingham had someone with him, a young woman, who pushed Benavidez over the cliff?"

"That's what Evan said."

Penny thought for a moment. "Do you suppose that it could have been her last night?"

"Well, I suppose it could have been but assuming she was twenty or so back then that would make her fifty by now. Kind of old to go around killing people." I said.

"I guess you're right, Vin. Besides, if it had been her, and she had waited that long, she would have had more to say than 'let me have a pack of cigarettes.' "

We sat and talked some more and then Penny yawned and said she was going to bed. I told her that I needed to study my notes and add to them.

"Oh, Vin, I am so sorry. It slipped my mind but I man called earlier for you."

"Yes?"

"Yes, he asked for you. Wouldn't give his name or a message except to say that he would call later." I had begun to develop my own connections, at Evan's direction, with individuals who might have information about the workings of the Southside. I encouraged them to call me at any time. Penny yawned again. "You know, Vin, you hardly got any sleep last night. You really should try to get some rest."

"Yes, I'll be there shortly." I said.

Penny stood at the door and looked back at me. "You have an idea about this, don't you Vin?"

"Yes." I smiled, realizing once again how difficult it was to hide my thoughts from Penny.

As Penny walked down the hallway toward the bedroom the telephone began to ring. I could hear her voice as she spoke to the person on the other end. When Penny returned to the kitchen, she was frowning. "A problem?" I asked. "Oh, Vin. That was Evan. He says that you are to go over and pick him up in twenty minutes."

"What happened, Penny?"

Penny bit her lower lip. "All Evan said was to tell you that Torres located the man from last night's shooting."

I showered quickly while Penny made the coffee.

— 16 —

Evan was standing under the portico of his mother's house when I drove up. He got into the passenger side. "Have you had any coffee, Vince?"

"Yes, Penny made some for us." I handed Evan the thermos. He poured a cup and lit a cigarette. I glanced over at him. He was wearing a fresh suit under his open trench coat and he looked quite alert.

"Where to, Evan?"

"Eighth and Florence." Evan took a drink of coffee and looked out of the window as I pulled out of the driveway. He turned to face me. "I got a call from your old partner, Pete Vereda." Evan paused. "He said he had tried to call you but there was no answer." I thought for a moment. "I thought I heard the telephone, Evan, but I was outside involved in a snowball fight." I said this lightly and smiled at Evan. Evan did not look at me. He looked straight ahead and said, "Pete didn't know what to do but I told him he was right in calling me. Right after Pete's call I got a call from Tommy."

I glanced over at Evan. His voice was different. "Pete was grabbing a bite over at his usual diner on Ochoa when he got a personal call. The person calling did not identify himself but told him that there was a body in an alley between Florence and Campbell." I thought about Pete, and why it would be so different to him about getting a call about a body. We got those calls all the time.

"So he went over to the location and there was the body. A man by the name of Fernando Obregon. Have you ever heard of him, Vince?" Evan turned to look at me.

I ran the name through my mind. I wanted to be sure before I answered. After a few moments I was able to connect the name with a face. If it was the same person, then yes, I did know him. He had been one of the people that Pete and I had questioned back at the time of the other murders. He had not been of any help and I had not known why he had been put on the list of people that the superiors wanted interviewed. He had been evasive but it had seemed to me that it was for a reason other than the murders. I also remembered that Pete had ridden him pretty hard, trying to get him to sweat but the man had remained cool. Evan spoke again. "He was a small time gambler, or so we thought, he may have been more deeply involved than we knew. He had a couple of old armed robberies on his sheet back when he was a juvenile. Hung out at the Blue Moon." Evan waited.

"Yes, Evan. I do remember him. He was one of the many people that we had been asked to interview back then."

"Have you had any contact with him since that time?" Evan turned to look at me. I thought again about Obregon but I was pretty sure that I had not seen him since then. "No, Evan."

"Okay, Vince, here is what I've heard so far." Evan poured himself another cup of the strong, black coffee. "Tommy picked up a lead across the river this afternoon. And then later he also got a call. He was told that Obregon had some information about who did Benavidez last night. Tommy was told where he could find Obregon but when he got there Pete was already there as a result of his own telephone call." Evan paused for a moment. An occasional snowflake landed on the windshield. There was no one about. The scotch had worn off and I felt jumpy.

"Now, this Obregon, has a bag with him and in that bag are a black dress and a black veil and a deck of cards…"

"A veil?" My question popped out. My nerves jangled about, and alarms went off in my head.

Evan glanced over at me. Apparently he thought I had missed some of his words, because he said, again, "Yes, a black dress, a black veil, and a deck of cards."

Something told me to tell Evan about the veil on the oleanders from the night before and I started to. "Evan…" I began, but Evan turned his head so quickly to look at me that it startled me. He was looking very intently at me. I reconsidered. Instead, I said, "I'm sorry, Evan, I didn't quite catch all of that the first time."

Evan continued to look at me. I focused my attention on the road. Evan lit another cigarette, and went on. "The deck of cards inside that bag was missing the ace of clubs." Evan did not speak for another block or so. He removed his hat and ran his hand through his hair. He began to speak and then stopped. We drove for another block, as the lights of the houses became dimmer and fewer.

"Vince, inside one of the man's pockets there was a notebook." I looked over at Evan. His words sounded strained. "There was a small notebook in which Obregon kept a record of his gambling accounts. Apparently he was also a bookie, running bets and payoffs back and forth across the bridge." Evan paused for just a moment. "And, Vince, in that book is your name."

I was not sure how I felt. I had never bet on anything in my whole life. Maybe it was another guy with my name. I shrugged. "Evan, that has to be a mistake. Or maybe there is some other Vincent Quiñones."

"No, Vince, Tommy doesn't think so. It has your telephone number."

Before I could stop myself, I raised my voice and said, "That is bullshit, Evan!"

We turned on Sixth and Evan told me to take a narrow side street with no name down to where there were several cars blocking our way. A police car was making its way back out in reverse. I moved over as far as I could and stopped the car and turned off the engine. Up ahead, coming from an alley, were the reflection of lights and the occasional flash of the cameras. I looked at my watch. It was a ten minutes of two in the morning. As the police car squeezed by us, I saw that Torres was on the passenger side. He seemed to restrain a smile as he looked at me and then with his fingers brushing his hat, he saluted Evan. Evan held up his hand for them to stop. I rolled down my window, as Torres rolled down his. Evan spoke to Torres. "Is everything intact over there, Tommy?" Torres smiled. He had perfect, white teeth. "Everything is intact, Number One." He looked at me, the smile now gone. "I'm on my way to see the Chief." Looking at me but speaking to Evan, Torres added, "By the way, Number One, someone needs to have a talk with Officer Vereda. He got a little frisky tonight." The car worked its way back to the end of the street, turned on its flashing lights, and sped away. Evan and I put on our gloves and stepped out of the car. As we walked up to the entrance to the alley, a reporter came out of it, still scribbling on his notebook. When he saw us, he turned around and went back in. Evan touched my elbow and said, "It might get sticky in there, Vince. Let me do the talking. Let your eyes miss nothing."

The reporters plus the usual amount of onlookers were being held back by a cordon strung across the narrow alley. The small crowd gave way as Evan and I passed through. I saw Octavio speaking rather animatedly with one of the uniformed officers. One of the reporters called out to me, "Any comment, Quiñones?" I looked in his direction and started to respond but again Evan touched me on the elbow and I said nothing.

The victim was sprawled on his side underneath a narrow wooden shelf that had been nailed into the adobe wall at the end of the blind alley. Six feet from the body an open door led into a house where there was no furniture that I could see. The victim's legs were in a puddle of water, and in one hand he held one of the wooden handles of a canvass satchel. The bag rested, partially open, on his left hip. I noticed that there was less snow on him than on the ground. Evan and I walked up close to the body. He was well dressed but with no hat or overcoat. As always when Evan studied a body, he would whisper a few words. I could never quite make them out, and I did not know whether they were some kind of benediction or a promise. The expression frozen into Obregon's face was one of surprise.

Evan reached down and removed the satchel from the man's loose grasp and handed it to me. I could see the black dress inside. Evan turned the body slightly, away from the wall. There was a knife stuck in the man's upper-left back, six inches below the shoulder, all the way to the hilt. I felt a brief, sharp pain in my own back as I saw this. As Evan turned the body, the man's hand slowly slipped from his side. He was wearing a diamond ring that flashed briefly in the light, and then his hand splashed down into the puddle of the ice-cold water. Two slow ripples radiated outward.

The man's suit jacket was open, and tucked into the waistband of his pants was a revolver. It was a snub-nose thirty-eight. Evan carefully removed it and called one of the officers over and handed it to him. The officer carried a large envelope with the date, time, and location on it upon which Evan made notations on the blank lines. The officer placed the revolver in the envelope and said, "Should I have someone call Bellamy, Evan?" Evan looked up at the officer. "No, let him sleep. This can wait until he arrives in the morning."

Evan searched the man's pockets. In the inside pocket of the man's jacket was his wallet. Evan opened it, as I shined my flashlight on it. The driver's license showed the victim's name as Fernando B. Obregon. His other piece of identification, the one that allowed him to go back and forth across the river, showed the same name with a birthplace of Parral, Mexico. I remembered the name of that town from Evan's story. I noticed that Evan studied each of the two photographs intently. There were three ticket stubs with numbers on them, a picture of a young woman, and another picture of that same woman, now older, holding a baby in her arms. There were also four twenty-dollar bills and two tens. Evan slipped the man's wallet back into the pocket and from the other side pocket Evan withdrew a black notebook. He handed it to me without opening it. At that moment a camera flashed, followed by about six others.

Evan spoke, still softly and only to me. The other officers, including Pete, who I had not noticed before, were standing in a group twenty feet away. "What do you think, Vinny?"

"No robbery, obviously." I said. "I think that he was stabbed in there and he made it out this far."

"And?" Evan looked at me.

"And, I think that this evidence was planted on him."

Evan stepped away and walked through the open doorway into the house. He came back in a matter of seconds and signaled for Teo Steele to come over. Evan asked him a question that I could not make out and Teo went over to the small crowd and brought back an elderly man who was shaking either from the cold or from nervousness. Teo told the man who we were and then he introduced the man to us as Don Mateo. Teo stepped back behind the man and made a sign for Evan by tapping one finger on his temple.

Evan led the old man into the house, out of the cold. We passed through the first room, which I had seen from the outside, and which was bare of any furniture. In an ordinary house this would be the kitchen, I assumed. I placed the satchel on a small table in the living room. That room held only the table, two chairs, and a very old couch over which was draped a man's overcoat and on one of the armrests was a man's hat. Evan introduced me a second time to the old man and then nodded to me in the direction of the couch. I searched the pockets of the overcoat. There was a pack of cigarettes in one pocket and a lighter and a single key on a chain in the other. From the living room, I could see three small rooms, in which there was a narrow bed and dresser in each. The house smelled of cheap perfume. The man told Evan that he owned that house but that it was vacant. He himself lived in the house next door, he said. Evan smiled at the man. The man then said that he did rent it out on a temporary basis, an afternoon here and an evening there.

"How about tonight? Any tenants tonight?" The man seemed relieved that Evan had used the word "tenants".

The man thought for a moment, unsure it seemed. "A woman, one I had not seen before, reserved it this afternoon for this evening, but she never showed up."

"Did you get a good look at her?"

"No, she stood across the street." The man paused, and then added, "She sent a boy with the money like they always do."

"The boy, do you know him?"

"No, never saw him before. Not from this neighborhood."

Evan considered the old man's words, and looked into the small rooms. "How do your tenants get the key?"

The man, who appeared peeved at the question and who was quite clearly senile, said, "The key is underneath a rock underneath a bush out there." The man pointed toward the front of the house.

"By the way, how was the woman dressed?" I asked

The old man looked at me with a puzzled look on his face, and then he looked at Evan and back at me. "Why, she was dressed in red, of course." His mouth moved as though he was laughing but no sound came out.

"These…" Evan paused, "reservations, are they for rooms or the house?"

"Both, either." The old man said. He then proceeded to explain his rates for *cama* and *casa* with much emphasis on the difference, as though he had forgotten to whom he was talking to and wanted no misunderstanding on his rates.

"So," Evan continued, "the boys bring the money to you and you tell them where they can find the key?" The old man seemed not to see any problem with this arrangement. In a gesture meant to signify his frustration, with the fingers on each hand touching, and with both hands held up close to his neck, the man said, "They all know where the key is. I get tired of telling them."

Evan looked at the old man and placed his hand on his shoulder. "Don Mateo, this is very important. Please think about this."

"Yes?" The man looked up into Evan's face. His eyes narrowed, and he seemed to concentrate.

"That man out there, did he come here often?"

The man thought about Evan's question. "There are so many, but him, no, never."

"How did he get here?" I asked.

"In a taxi." The old man looked at me. It occurred to me that the old man might be mistaken since the address in the victim's wallet had been at a location just a little over a block away.

"Are you sure, sir?" I asked.

The old man looked at me. "Who can be sure of anything, young man?"

I moved on. "Was the woman already here? Waiting for him?"

"No, I don't think she ever showed up. She may have, though."

"Did you see another man arrive?" I asked.

"I did not see any other person arrive. I do not see everyone who comes and goes. It was dark, and snowing." The old man waved in the direction of the alley without taking his eyes off of me. "Then, they started to argue."

"Who started to argue?"

"The two men, the two policemen."

Evan again placed his hand on the old man's shoulder. "What where they arguing about, Don Mateo?"

"About the dead man, and about what he had in his pockets. A reporter showed up and then another. The two policemen were in the alley, arguing, and then they came in here, where they had asked me to wait." The old man looked at me and then at Evan. "I thought that they were going to get into a fight right here."

"What were they arguing about, sir?" I repeated Evan's question.

The old man looked at me. "Did you say that your name was Quiñones?"

"Yes." I said.

"Well, they were arguing about you."

Evan reached into his pocket and brought out his pack of cigarettes and lit one as he studied the walls of the living room. Then he said, "And this you told to the reporters, Don Mateo?"

"And this I told to the reporters." The old man said, bobbing his head up and down in confirmation.

Evan spoke slowly to the old man. "Don Mateo, this is a crime scene. You are not to rent it nor enter it again until you are told to do so by a police officer. Also, it would be in your best interest if you were not to discuss this matter with anyone. Do you understand what I am saying?" The man said that he understood perfectly and doddered out the front door.

17

After the man was gone, Evan gave me a sad smile and then he sat down on one of the chairs. With one slow motion he spilled out the contents of the satchel. There was a dress, hat, veil, and a deck of cards still in a box. Evan looked at the trademark on the box but did not open it. He began rubbing his eyes and as he rubbed them he asked me to describe the contents of the notebook for him. I remained standing as I took the small, leather-bound black book out of my pocket.

The book contained page after page of neatly printed entry-filled columns. The first column had no names but three-digit numbers. The next column had the contest; which included horse races, soccer games, baseball games, and boxing matches. Then, the odds with a slash and the amount of the bet. In some of the entries for the amount of the bet there was a plus sign with another amount that appeared at a glance to be five percent of the amount wagered. In the last column was the amount paid out. Some of the bets were for considerable amounts. I described to Evan what I was seeing in the book. I did not see my name on any page.

On the back cover of the book there was a pocket from which a folded piece of paper stuck out. I removed the paper and opened it. That piece of paper was of a different type than the rest of the sheets in the book. The note had my last name and telephone number. Below that was the name and address of the grocery store and then the amount of one thousand dollars, followed by a subtraction of five hundred dollars leaving a balance of five hundred. I compared the writing on the note with the writing in the rest of the book. They looked to be the same. I had the need to sit down.

I sat across from Evan and slid the note and the notebook across the table to him. Evan glanced at the two items but did not say anything, although a slight frown did appear on his face. Finally, I had to ask the question. "What do you think of this, Evan?" Evan must have seen the worried look on my face. He laughed softly. "Why, I think we have a case here, Vinny." I laughed also, although my laugh was dry. Almost as a reflex my hand reached out and I picked up the veil and smelled it. If anything it smelled of laundry soap, as if it had been recently washed.

Evan began putting the articles back into the satchel as he spoke. "By the way, Vinny. Bellamy told me that you had turned in a black veil yesterday morning." I knew that each piece of encoded evidence in any particular case would be consolidated in one location and that the person who did the consolidating would be one of Bellamy's assistants. I knew that sooner or later Evan would know about the veil. Now I kicked myself for not having told Evan about it right away.

"Yes, Evan. I wasn't sure if it had anything to do with last night's homicide. I found it attached to the oleanders back along the canal." Evan gave me a look of chastisement, which only he could deliver. "I am sorry, Evan." I added. Bellamy must have told Evan about my note on the evidence envelope because he now asked, "Did you catch any scent on our victim out there?"

"Yes."

"What was it?"

"It seemed to be Barrington's, Evan."

Evan reached into his pockets, looking for something. "Do you have any tags, Vinny?" I pulled out a tag with the attached string. I filled in the information on the tag and secured it to the closed handles of the satchel. As I was doing this, Evan spoke. "One time, back when I first became Bellamy's partner, I always had the idea that I would find some small piece of evidence that would solve a case. I was always on the lookout for such an item. So much so that I was taking in too much stuff. You know, when you come right down to it a guy could haul away everything from a crime scene including the kitchen sink. Who knows but that the perpetrator might have washed his hands there and there could be some blood in the trap." I looked at Evan. He smiled at me. He was describing exactly how I felt. "So, one day, about fifty feet away from where the victim had been shot, I found an empty pack of cigarettes. I hesitated. Should I inventory this or not? What will Bellamy think? Well, I picked it up and noticed that it had been opened from the bottom instead of the top. I walked over to Bellamy and showed it to him. Bellamy said, 'that's just great, Morrow, that narrows it down to the ten thousand men in El Paso who smoke that brand.' So I turned it over to show him how it had been opened. 'I'll be damned.' Bellamy said. It just so happened that Bellamy knew a man who opened his cigarettes that way. A quirk. And the man who did this had indeed witnessed the crime but did not want to get involved until Bellamy coaxed it out of him."

I felt relieved and also the need to explain further. "Evan, so much happened last night and the veil—"

Evan held up his hand. "You don't need to explain, Vince. We do what we do." Evan's words were clear enough but the tone of his voice told me that this should not happen again. Then his tone changed back to normal and he said, "I think we should hear what Pete has to say." I walked back out to the alley and waved for Pete to come inside. He walked in quickly and sat down on the chair at the table opposite Evan while I sat on the couch.

"That sonofabitch." Pete said. His face was flushed.

"Calm down, Pete." Evan said this as a direct order. "Tell us what happened." Evan took out his pack of cigarettes and placed it on the table next to the black book.

Pete glanced over at me and then back at Evan. "I'm at the diner on Ochoa and the waitress comes over and tells me that I have a call. A man, muffled voice and all that shit, tells me that there is a body here. I come over. Come up the alley in my car. There are two reporters out there hanging around the body already and I tell them to get the hell away from there. The door is open so I come inside this here cathouse and sitting there on the couch is the old man, shaking away, looking strange. I think that he is the one who did the deed so I draw my gun but at that same time Torres comes walking in the front door with his gun drawn also. He doesn't say shit to me or to the old man but walks through here and out to the alley. He goes through the guy's pockets and pulls out that book. 'Oh, shit.' He says. What is it? I ask him. 'Take a look.' Torres says. 'Look at the name in here." Pete glanced over at me and said, "I'm sorry, partner." I nodded my head, for him to go on.

"Well, I guess I lose my head and he and I get into an argument. I tell him that the piece of paper doesn't mean shit, that we should just ignore it and let you, Evan, decide what kind of bullshit is going on. He asks me if I am suggesting that we withhold evidence. Well, that really gets me going and I tell him so. Then we come in here and argue some more." Pete paused and then looked in my direction. "One of these days me and that sonofabitch are going to get together off duty." As Pete was speaking, a thought flashed through my mind. I wondered if perhaps the fact that Pete and Torres were both from the Southside but from different barrios made them natural enemies. I looked at the agitation on Pete's face and my thoughts went back to the time he had saved my life.

He and I had been walking down the street when a woman, clearly deranged, walked toward us and gave me a strange look. She walked by and then, quick as a cat, she had lunged at me with a ten-inch dagger. Pete, ever alert, had deflected the blade just as it tore into the back of my shirt. The woman was amazingly strong, and it had taken both of us to subdue her. The dagger had gone in about an inch and a half just behind my heart.

Now, Evan sighed a sigh much like that of a father in the midst of quarreling sons. In fact, Evan's expression was the same one that I had seen on my own father's face in those situations.

Evan leaned slightly toward Pete. "Pete, what you do off duty is your own business. But while you are on duty and dealing with a homicide, especially, you will keep your head. Your outburst around that old man will cost us." Evan's eyes bored into Pete's, and I had a vision of what the headlines would be in the morning. Pete rubbed his forehead and apologized again. He looked at me and said, "Who would want to do this to you, Vince?" A wave of anger rushed through me and I was suddenly not tired in the least. Pete came over and shook my hand on his way back out. I remained on the couch and tried to think who might want to do this. I looked at Evan, who had opened the book and seemed to be studying the pages. I wondered if perhaps he was memorizing it, a particular feat that I had seen him do before and one that astounded me. My own mind was racing in every direction. Evan closed the black book and then he took out his own notebook and wrote in it. Evan turned to look at me and said, "There is smoke here, Vince." As he spoke those words, Teo walked in and handed Evan a slip of paper. "From Octavio." Teo said. "He said it was very important." Evan read the note, and I watched his head go back just enough to be noticeable.

Evan looked at the note again. He slipped it into his pocket and then spoke to Teo. "Tell Toby I will talk to him in fifteen minutes." Then Evan lit a cigarette and turned to me and said, "What do we have here, Vince?"

Evan looked at me, waiting. I came back from my own dark thoughts, subdued my anger, and began. "Evan, I think that our victim was lured here for a good reason. In the fashion that he is dressed I think that he didn't come here for the usual. I would say that it was to pay off a large bet or to take one in." I waited for Evan to display some kind of encouragement to me but he had removed the tag on the satchel and was looking into it again. He removed the dress and held it up in front of him, as though he was checking the size. I went on. "Whoever did last night's homicide is here waiting for him and that person has the satchel and gun." Evan looked up at me and said, "Yes, Vinny, I have no doubt that the revolver on our victim out there will prove to be the one used on Benavidez." Then, with a wave of his hand Evan prompted me to continue. I told Evan I thought that tonight's killer wanted us to believe that last night's killer was hired to do the job and then was himself killed tonight to silence him and close the loop. Evan smiled at me. "Yes, but that is a lot of money to pay someone, Vinny. You could have gotten someone to do it for fifty dollars." I tried to smile also but it was probably a grimace. My jaw felt very tight.

"There are flaws in what the killer was trying to present to us, right Vinny? First of all, why would last night's perpetrator be carrying around this self-incriminating evidence and still hold on to that bag after he had been stabbed in the back and obviously running for his life?" Evan did not wait for my answer, which was just as well because I didn't have one. "So, at first glance, one could assume that it was planted." Evan looked out of the open door toward the alley. "But it is almost too evident, Vince. Hell, the killer might just as well have left us a note attached to the body telling us so. And, he did leave a note. A note implicating you, Vince." Evan looked at me and smiled. "I have no doubt that you could throw a stick up in the air in this part of the city and it would land on a passable forger who could create that note for a quarter." I felt strange, a mixture of discomfort and anger. Evan paused. "Now, after the deed is done what does the killer do? He goes to a telephone and makes at least three calls. A newspaper for one. You will recall that the newspapers had a wonderful time with us during the period of the other three murders. And then he calls someone close to each of us. Namely, your ex-partner and my ex-partner. Why them, I wonder?" Evan took a puff of his cigarette. "So, last night's killer wanted us to believe that it was a Club of Clubs deal and tonight's killer wants us to believe that you were involved. I am tempted to discard these two illusions out of hand except for the fact that behind those illusions hides the truth." Evan paused and his face grew pensive. "But let's look at the grocery store homicide first, Vin. Tell me what we know."

I tried to forget my feelings and concentrated on the task at hand. I ran the facts about the previous night's murder quickly through my mind and began. "We know from the eyewitness that at ten o'clock a man dressed as a woman walked into the store, spoke a few words, and shot the owner in the chest with a .38 caliber pistol. The killer placed the ace of clubs on the counter, and the killer left the store without taking any money from the cash register. We also know that the victim had a trunk buried under the kitchen floor. We know that it was empty except for two gold coins." Evan held up his hand and gave me a sad smile. "Even an old detective can misread the facts, Vin. Suppose, just for the sake of argument, that it was a woman. A woman with a deep voice. And suppose that the trunk had been empty for some time. After all, that gold would have been in Benavidez' possession for over thirty-some years. He could have spent it all before." Evan paused, and into that pause I repeated Penny's words. "But Evan, why would Benavidez bury an empty trunk?" After a moment or two Evan responded. "Perhaps that was merely a force of habit. Who knows? There are stranger things, Vin. There are some crime scenes, where, as you know, articles appear as though from thin air. The relative or friend of the victim will proclaim quite strongly that he or she has never seen that particular item and that it does not belong there. It can be anything— a strange book, a hairbrush, an article of clothing. Yet, at the end of the investigation, the killer himself will tell us that he did not bring it." Evan was right. He and I had investigated a homicide where the male victim had been strangled to death in his living room and there in plain sight was a pair of woman's shoes still in an open box. They were brand new and they were red. No one knew how they had gotten there, including the killer, and in the end those shoes didn't have anything to do with anything. "So, Vinny, if robbery was not the motive what do we have left?"

Evan's question brought me up short. If last night's homicide had not had anything to do with robbery then my theory was shot to hell. It meant that Rosalinda and Torres were not an item and Benny had been merely scared as he himself had told me. It also meant that the veil had blown onto the oleanders from God knows where and the scent on it didn't mean a damn thing as far as these two investigations were concerned. Everything was changed if there was no gold in the trunk. A part of me welcomed this possibility while another part of me could not.

Evan waited for my response. I moved back to the thrust of what Evan was proposing. "Evan, if it was not robbery, then we are left with a Club murder, or, a murder which had nothing to do with the Club of Clubs but was meant to appear that way."

"Yes we are, Vin. That is what is left." Evan took out his notebook and seemed to look for a particular page. He glanced at it and then put his notebook away. "I would like to sleep on this, Vinny, and I might feel differently afterwards but for now…" Evan hesitated and then looked at me. "Check me out on this." It was the first time that Evan had ever asked me to check him out on anything.

"If you will recall, Bellamy arrived at the conclusion that Miss Lucero had a lover. Now, yesterday afternoon, before our meeting, I had gone back to the holding center to see her but she was of no help since she could not utter a full sentence without breaking down in tears." At the mention of Rosalinda's name I felt the twinge of something in my stomach. An image of Rosalinda in tears came to me and I felt great pity for her. I lost track of Evan's words momentarily and then I tuned in again. "…not be the first time. But suppose that there was a lover involved here but not in the way that Bellamy was thinking?" Evan stopped and looked away from me. "And suppose, Vinny, that the fifth man, the fifth member of the *bastos*, the one that Bellamy said had already departed, was still alive? And suppose further that the reason he was still alive was because he was Benavidez' lover?"

I looked at Evan, I could feel my eyes blinking. Evan's words had yanked me back from a totally different path. It was not so much the content of what Evan was saying but rather the direction in which he was headed that brought me up short. I had seen many an occasion back home in San Francisco where two elderly homosexuals could still treat each other with the utmost affection. The couple who had lived next door to us had indeed displayed that same emotion. And, sometimes they even fought much the same as a husband and wife, one jealous of the other's behavior. Yes, anything was possible. "And suppose further, Vinny, that this murder was merely a matter of revenge." Evan slumped back slightly in his chair, as though knocked off balance by the implications of his own words. I could see that he was not comfortable with the subject of homosexual lovers. Seeking to relieve his apparent discomfort, I told Evan about Larry and Bill, our neighbors back home, who were both in their sixties, and how they acted toward one another. I told him that they had been professional dancers in their youth and that they owned a dance studio and gave dance lessons and how they had given Penny and me a complete set of very expensive china, and how they had danced up a storm at our wedding. It was a night of firsts, it seemed to me, since after I said that to Evan he looked at me with what appeared to be a faint look of appreciation.

Evan exhaled and continued. "Okay, Vince, since that is a possibility at the least, let us assume that our victim here was last night's killer and suppose that he had not been paid at all but did it for his own purposes. And then Benavidez'…lover, the fifth member of the club, finds out who it is and then kills him as an act of revenge." Evan looked at me, prompting me to respond. I had several points to dispute but I could not bring myself to say them since it had taken Evan, it seemed to me, great effort to voice this theory.

During any investigation in which we were involved, except those that were cut and dried, Evan and I might run through a set of theories until we could agree on the one that would most closely fit the facts. It was a matter of understanding the *how* to arrive at the *why* to hopefully lead us to the *who*. Usually, our thinking was pretty close but if we were far apart one of us would challenge the other. Evan encouraged this. And in this case I was not sure if Evan was merely offering this theory for me to question or whether he had settled on it, but while he had been talking my mind had been traveling a mile a minute in a very different direction. I was glad that Evan seemed to be giving little credence to the fact that my name was in that book. But still it was my name and no one else's and that made it very personal for me. As far as I was concerned it was a little piece of bullshit thrown in for my benefit. To my way of thinking the person who put my name in there had to have known that it would aggravate me. So, yes, I had my own theory and it was quite different from Evan's. And, if only a few hours before my theory had been a mere skeleton now it had begun to grow muscles. Still, and this was the hell of it, I had mixed emotions about the whole matter. I had to admit that I dreaded the implications of my own hunch. Now, I had to either voice my theory or go in Evan's direction.

My decision to follow Evan's direction was influenced by a brief flash that I had had as Bellamy was speaking the previous afternoon, and that was that the fifth man had some bearing on the matter. And then, later, it had occurred to me that the barber, Don Jose, in Evan's story was probably that fifth man. Yes, it had also crossed my mind as Bellamy had made his diagrams on the blackboard in Evan' office that if Octavio's explanation was a possibility, that is, that a vendetta could be passed down from one generation to the next, then it could have been a son of one of the original three victims. I remembered Bellamy's words from another time. Sometimes, he had said, when we clutch at straws we find the needle in the haystack. Now, Evan looked at me.

I let my mind go and the words followed. "If there is no robbery then that changes everything. Say that a son of one of the original victims from three years ago finds out that Benavidez is the person who killed his father. I don't think that it would have been that person himself because of the words that he spoke. If it had been that person he would have said something like 'you are the sonofabitch that killed my father.' But if that person hired the killer then the killer would not have had to say anything." I waited for Evan to speak but he merely waved me on. I took a deep breath. "So, that would make tonight's victim the hired killer and the fifth man finds out and lures him here." My thoughts raced even farther out. "Now, tonight's killer knows that our victim out there was hired by someone and wants to find out who, so he puts out the word that he will pay one thousand dollars for that information and our guy out there comes forward. In this case he is thinking that he will be paid twice, by two different individuals, for the same crime. Tonight's killer gives him five hundred but wants more proof, namely, the disguise. So, our victim puts the disguise in the satchel and agrees to meet him here—" Abruptly, Evan stopped me. "Vin, in your opinion, do you think that one lover could kill the other? Or have him killed?"

As I had been speaking I had had the hint of an altogether different thought about the thousand dollars and my name in the book. It had been brief and exciting, like the flash of gold in a pan. Now I thought about Evan's question. I told Evan that what was surprising about homosexuals was that they were just like the rest of us, only different. Could they kill out of passion? Yes, of course. Could they have a lover killed? "On that part all I can say is that whatever is possible in society in general is possible in the world of homosexuals."

Evan did not ask me any more questions. He sat in his chair and smoked his cigarette. Outside, the occasional snowflake still fell. After Evan was finished with his cigarette he turned to me and said, "Vin, Toby thinks that this victim is the son of one of the *carteros*. He may have been killed for no other reason than that."

Evan stood up and walked over and picked up the victim's overcoat. "Vinny, I am going to listen to what Toby has to say now." He took out the key and handed it to me. "What I would like you to do is walk down to Obregon's house. According to his papers it is close by. Go out through the front door here and avoid the reporters. See what you can find out but do not remove any item. I will send someone to pick you up from there later."

—— 18 ——

There were no reporters on the front side of the house. I crossed the street and walked down to the end of the next alley. There was no one about. I walked past Obregon's house and then came back toward it. The small house sat in the shadows at the end of a narrow yard, back away from the streetlight. Just as I was about to turn and go in through the old open gate, I saw a car coming slowly down the street. I continued walking past the house and on down the street and then I stopped in the darkness beyond the light. A taxi stopped at the gate. The cab driver got out and helped a woman dressed in black out of the back of the taxi and then he walked by her side to the door of the house. I heard the sound of their words but could not make them out. The cab driver came back to his taxi and drove off.

I waited half a minute or so before I walked up to the door and knocked. A voice came from behind the door. "Who is it?"

"I am Detective Quiñones. May I come in?" The door opened slightly. In the dim light I could not tell whether the woman was young or old but her voice was soft as she spoke to me. "I have been informed. The police have already been here."

"I am sorry, miss, was that your husband?" After a long moment, as though the question had confused her, she finally responded. "No, my brother." A sob came from her lips and then another.

"Please, miss, let me in. I am very sorry about your brother but I must ask you some questions." The door opened all the way and as I stepped across the threshold the woman fell into my arms, trembling and crying. I held her in the darkness and after a few moments she moved away and turned on the lamp by the door. I looked at her young, tear-stained face. She turned away from me but not before I had seen in her eyes the dim, faraway look of a blind person. She moved slowly to the couch and sat down. "Please, Detective Quiñones, have a seat." She reached over to the small table by the couch and felt around for a pair of tinted glasses and put them on. "My name is Teresa." She smiled in my direction and began to sob again, caught herself, and then said, "I am sorry, how may I help you?"

"Teresa, I apologize for the circumstances. I am truly sorry about your brother."

"I believe that you are, Detective Quiñones. May I offer you some coffee?"

"Yes, thank you, but please call me Vince." Thinking that she would need help in the kitchen, I added, "May I help you make it?"

"Oh no, not necessary." Teresa stood up and walked toward the open kitchen area. I watched her movements as she started the coffee. They were as sure as a sighted person. I glanced away from Teresa and quickly took in the rest of the room. It was very neat and clean. Occupying more than half of the wall to my right was a large bookcase. Most of the books on the shelves were large and thick. As I looked at the books more closely I could make out the upraised dots on their spines indicative of Braille. On the lowest shelf there were regular sized books with readable titles, most of them in Spanish.

I wondered how I should go about questioning Teresa about her brother and I began by saying to her as gently as I could, "Teresa, it pains me to have to ask you any questions tonight but when was the last time that you saw your brother?" Teresa lit a match and placed it over the open jet of one of the burners of the stove. The blue flame of the gas sprang to life. Teresa took the burning match and extinguished it by placing it under the running water of the faucet in the sink. She turned to face me and said, "Would you like to sit at the table?" I walked over and pulled out one of the two chairs from the table and held it out for her while I placed my hand lightly on her elbow. She turned slightly and took one of my hands into hers and moved the tips of her fingers over the palm of my hand. I don't know what this meant or what she could tell about me by merely touching my hand but she made a sound that seemed to be one of satisfaction. She sat down and I sat across from her at the table. Teresa sat composed and perfectly straight and placed her hands with her fingers interlocking on the table.

"Do you think that my brother was a bad person?"

"No, Teresa, I think that the person who did this is the bad person and I need your help in finding out who that might be."

"Fernando was a good person. He began running bets back and forth across the bridge at age twelve, did you know that?"

"No." I said. I did not want to get into a long conversation about the victim's life but I was determined to go along if that meant I could get some current information.

"Yes. He did it to help support me. He always said that it was only until he could save enough money for us to move back to Parral and reopen the bookstore that our mother had there."

My ears perked up. "You are from Parral?"

"Yes. Fernando and I were born there although from different fathers. Fernando never knew his father. His father was killed in a mining town in Arizona before mother gave birth."

Teresa's words startled me and I must have made some sound in my throat or made some audible movement in my chair because Teresa said, "You are surprised at this?"

I was surprised of course because this fact might go a long way in deflating my own theory but I did not want to influence Teresa one way or the other. Now I said as simply as I could, "It is a fact that might be helpful to us, Teresa."

"Yes," Teresa continued, "it was a fact that interested me also but mother never wanted to say too much about it. You, I'm sure, are familiar with the way someone will try to steer a conversation away from something that they would like to keep to themselves."

"Yes, of course."

"At first she told us that Fernando's father was killed in a mining accident. But her voice sounded different whenever she said that. It was as though she was trying very hard to sound matter-of-fact." Teresa smiled. "It was almost like a game. It became a great mystery for me. The thought of the life of my mother as a young woman before she married my father filled me with curiosity. The more I felt that she was trying to keep something from me the more determined I became to find out what it was. I would ask her for details concerning her first husband's death and one time she would paint it one way and then later it would be slightly different. You know, she could have told me at any time that she had answered all of my questions and not get into it any further but she never did." Teresa paused and sighed deeply. "I do not remember mother ever being sick and then, when I was thirteen, she was told by her doctor that she had only a short time to live. My father had also died suddenly two years before. It was in the spring and she packed us a lunch and we rode our horses out to the country and had a picnic. It was then that she told me the whole story." Teresa brushed away a tear from the corner of one eye. "You are aware, Vince, that Villa had women soldiers in his army?"

"Yes, Teresa, I have heard that. Your mother was a soldier in the revolution?"

"Yes, she was. That is where she met Fernando's father."

As we drank our coffee, Teresa told me a tale that corroborated much of Evan's story but with much more detail. She told me that her mother had arrived first in the town of Santa Rosa and that she had gotten a job as a maid in the hotel there. Later, Fernando's father had arrived. They were searching for a man named Benavidez who had stolen a great deal of gold from Villa's treasury. However, it was apparent that Teresa's mother believed Benavidez had been killed. She had not known Benavidez had survived the fall.

At this point I asked Teresa if her mother had ever described Benavidez for her. "Yes, she said that he was a homosexual and that he spoke like a woman and posed as one."

"Anything else?"

"Mother said that the little finger on his left hand was missing. She said that his finger had been bitten off by a woman."

"Teresa, that man who your mother thought that she had killed actually survived the fall. He was arrested but escaped. We are fairly certain that he is the man who killed those other three men here three years ago."

Through the lightly tinted glasses I could see Teresa's eyes blink rapidly and then move from side to side. As my words sank in, Teresa's hand came up quickly to cover her mouth. It seemed to me that a powerful thought had passed through her mind. "It is not possible, Vince." Teresa's words were a mere whisper.

"Teresa, we are pretty sure about that."

"No, I believe that that part is true. But if you are here because you think that Fernando killed the man from the grocery store, that is not possible. Fernando could never do anything like that."

I wanted to pursue that angle in spite of Teresa's objections. "Teresa, your brother had the clothes in a satchel with him. The clothes that fit the description of the disguise worn at the time. In that bag there was a deck of cards with the ace of clubs missing. "

I could see that Teresa's hands had begun to tremble. I plunged ahead. "Teresa, is there something else you would like to tell me?" Teresa grew silent, as though she had retreated deep into her own thoughts. I looked out of the window behind her. A difference in the darkness hinted at the dull light of dawn. Teresa came back, speaking softly. "The radio said that the person who killed the grocer was dressed in a black dress, hat, and veil. And then Fernando read me the article in the paper and that is what it said also."

"Yes, that is correct."

"And you say that Fernando had those articles in a bag?"

"Yes, that is what we found."

"Did you see the veil?"

"I did, Teresa."

Teresa took a deep breath and sighed as she exhaled. "Was the veil torn?" I was surprised at Teresa's question. I had not seen any tear on either the one I had found on the oleanders nor on the one in the satchel. "No, Teresa, but why do you ask?"

Once again Teresa grew pensive and once again she came back speaking softly, almost in a whisper. "I had only one black veil. It had been given to me by my mother. Early yesterday Fernando told me that he had noticed that it was torn and he went out and bought me a new one. I told him that I would wear the new one but that I also wanted to keep the old one."

My heart skipped a beat. "This was after he read you the article?"

"Yes, and then he took the old one and said that he knew a seamstress who might be able to mend it."

The thought that had excited me as Evan and I had spoken earlier, now began to rattle about in my head. I forced myself to remain calm. "Teresa, did Fernando mention anything to you about coming into a large sum of money?"

Teresa stiffened. "What are you getting at?"

"Teresa, please, I am making no accusations here."

I could see the sudden slump in Teresa's shoulders. She removed her glasses and cried into her hands. "Oh, Fernando why?...why?" I stood up and took out my handkerchief. I touched one of Teresa's hands and then placed it there. She opened the handkerchief and sobbed softly into it. I waited a moment or two and then I pressed on.

"Teresa, did Fernando ever mention my name to you?" Teresa, composed again, folded my handkerchief and handed it back to me.

"No, I do not think so."

"The reason I ask this is because my name and telephone number were in the book where he kept the information on betting." I looked at Teresa, hoping that she might have some idea why my name would be in that book. She brushed her dark hair away from her shoulders but she did not speak. I went on. "Did he mention any other name in the police department?" There must have been something in my voice when I asked that question because a quizzical look came upon Teresa's face. Then, there was the faintest of smiles. "No, no names, but he did say that some of them liked to gamble." Teresa paused a moment. "Do you, Vince?"

I thought about Teresa's question. I had to admit that there had been times in my life when I had gambled. There was no doubt about it. There had been times when I had taken chances in affairs of the heart and lost every time. I laughed. "Not on contests." I said.

Teresa made a gesture with her hands open. "I was born with vision and I remember all the colors and the faces of every person I knew. After mother died things began to grow dim. It happened very quickly. The doctors told me that as my vision left, my other senses would become quite acute. They were right. If all else is quiet, I can hear the sound of someone writing across the room, and some voices are so rich that they create shadows." I don't know why Teresa was telling me this but her words jolted me. I felt at that moment that she knew me quite well with only the sound of my voice. I understood her words to say that my voice was me, and that I should take care in what I said. I sat upright and said, "I believe you, Teresa." I scribbled a few notes and I was surprised to hear the scratching sound of pencil on paper. I had never noticed that sound before. I then told Teresa that in her brother's book some entries were shown as numbers instead of names. I asked her if she knew who the people were that those numbers signified. She said that she could not help me in that regard. "Teresa, I am sure that Fernando was quite discreet about his business but did he happen to mention to you any particular individual who lost a large amount here within the past couple of months or so?"

"No, he never talked much about those things." Teresa stood up and walked to the stove. She picked up the coffeepot and brought it back to the table where she asked me to lift my cup and then, holding my hand in hers, she poured me a full cup without spilling a drop. She poured herself another cup and returned the pot back to the stove. When she came back to the table she spoke again almost in a whisper. "Vince, whatever Fernando did I think he did for me. He knew that it was my dream to return to Parral and reopen mother's store." I looked at Teresa's young face. She could not be any older than nineteen. I wondered what would become of her now that she had lost her brother. I too, softened my voice. "Yes, Teresa, of that I am sure."

"You asked me if Fernando mentioned something about coming into money?"

"Yes, Teresa."

"Well, he did. Just yesterday. But it was strange."

"Strange? In what way, Teresa?"

"Well, he would place his own bets now and then. Usually not, but once in a while he would. But whenever he won, or anyone else won for that matter, they would be paid the full amount. Yesterday he told me that he had won a big bet but that he would be paid in two payments."

"Did you believe this, Teresa?"

"No. And I said so. I had a bad feeling about it. He laughed and told me that I should start packing because when he got his second payment we would be on our way back to Parral."

For a moment I wondered if the one hundred dollars that I had seen in Fernando's wallet could be a part of the so-called first payment. It did not seem to be a large amount in my view but I knew that it could be in someone else's eyes.

"Teresa, in Fernando's wallet there was one hundred dollars. Could that be the first payment?"

"One hundred dollars?"

"Yes."

"No, I wouldn't think so. He carried that amount usually with him. Some people had credit with him and he would cover their small bets. He would also lend money."

"Teresa, did Fernando have a girlfriend or some other close friend?"

"Many girlfriends but no close man friends. I suppose that I was his best friend."

"So, please, if you could tell me, Teresa, when was the last time that you saw your brother?"

"Yesterday, in the afternoon, I made his lunch and he sat at this very table."

"Did he tell you if he was meeting someone in the evening? Anything like that?"

"Yes, he said that he was going to meet with someone at 8:00."

I braced myself. "Did he say who that person was?" Teresa paused. I was not sure if she paused because she knew and did not want to tell me or because she was trying to remember. "No, he did not say but it seemed to me that whoever it was it was different."

"Different? In what way, Teresa?"

"Well, usually Fernando was very talkative but yesterday he was quiet as though he had something on his mind." For a moment Teresa seemed on the verge of losing her composure but then she regained it. I touched her hand and once again placed my handkerchief into it. She held it but did not open it or use it. She reached into her pocket, pulled out a slip of paper, and pushed it across the table. I opened it. It was a receipt from a bank in Juarez showing a transfer of forty thousand pesos on behalf of Fernando Obregon from them to a bank in Parral. I quickly calculated that at the monetary exchange rate that amount would be about five hundred American dollars. The thing that jumped out at me from the receipt was that it was for gold coin.

I made a note of the bank and the amount and the date. "Teresa, I am going to ask you not to show this receipt nor mention it to anyone else."

"Yes, all right."

"Do you know where Fernando was the night before last?"

Teresa sighed. "Vince, is it hopeless for Fernando?"

"I'm sorry?"

"Is it so hopeless for Fernando since everything points to him?"

"Again, Teresa, I am making no accusations."

"Yes, so you say. But you also say that the incriminating articles were found on him. And then you tell me that the grocer who was killed was the man who killed Fernando's father. What is it that you call that? A motive? Then, you ask about money and there it is. A receipt for five hundred dollars. So, is it hopeless?"

"Teresa, I must see this through. The two payments could signify that Fernando was paid by someone to kill the grocer. Maybe that is the way it was. Five hundred dollars down and—"

"Or?"

"I'm sorry?"

"Vince, I can hear the 'or' in your voice."

"I am not aware of any other explanation, Teresa."

"Yes you are. You believe that there is something else."

"Please, Teresa, I think that you are reading more into my voice than is really there."

The color sprang up to Teresa's cheeks and her lips clamped together. She crossed her arms tightly about her chest. Her indignation was evident. It struck me that to question her conclusion of the sound of my voice was equal to calling her a liar. I had the feeling that unless I admitted to her that I did indeed have my doubts about her brother our conversation was over. I looked once again at the window behind her where it was a little less dark than before. "It will be morning soon." I said. Teresa did not respond but simply kept her arms crossed about her. Her lips turned downward. "Please, Teresa." Nothing. She had retreated quite far away from me. I made a slurping sound with the last sip of coffee in my cup and waited to see if she would get up to refill it. She made no movement.

I sighed. "Very well, Teresa. This is what I think." Teresa came back. Her face lit up with victory. "I could be way off, you understand." I added.

"No, I do not believe that you could be *way* off." Teresa rose and brought back the coffeepot and poured me another cup. Her hand on mine felt feverish.

"I have my doubts about whether your brother had anything to do with the murder of Benavidez. The man who did it did not speak any words that would indicate revenge. However, your brother is not absolved completely." I waited for Teresa to object but she made no sound or gesture. I paused for a moment. Earlier I had remembered the man who had pretended to be drunk; the man who had told Evan about the woman in black running down the street. It had occurred to me as Evan and I had discussed tonight's murder that if the drunk had seen the woman in black running away why not someone else? What if someone else had seen the killer? And then, this night, I had wondered why Fernando had taken Teresa's veil after the fact.

I went on, not sure if I was really speaking to Teresa or if it was to hear the reasonableness of my own thoughts. "Suppose that Fernando saw the man who killed Benavidez? Yes, he sees the man run out of the store and follows him. The wind has blown the veil away. Your brother sees the man's face. Knows who he is. Fernando sees the man discard the disguise and the gun and retrieves those articles and brings them back here. In the morning he reads that there was a black veil also so he takes yours to make the evidence complete. Then, he contacts the killer and makes his demand. A thousand dollars or I go to the police. The killer stalls him. Says he can only pay five hundred. Needs more time for the other half. Then, after the killer has his own plan, he tells your brother to meet him someplace but that he will only pay him the rest if he brings the articles with him."

Teresa frowned. I was disappointed. If my theory did not sound reasonable even to a person who believed wholeheartedly that her brother was incapable of murder who was left that I could convince? "Are my words so unreasonable to you, Teresa?"

Teresa smiled faintly. "No, not at all. I think that you are right. I heard Fernando come in night before last. I heard him fumble around with the lock on the door, something that I had never heard him do before even when he had been drinking. And then I heard him pacing in his room for a long time. No, what you have said makes sense to me. But knowing that he was dealing with a killer, and knowing that my brother was a cautious person, why did he not take steps to protect himself?"

"Do you mean some type of insurance?"

"Yes, something like that."

"I was hoping that he had told you something, Teresa. Or left something for you. A letter, perhaps." I knew that the chances were slim that Fernando would have verbally told Teresa anything about his scheme. There was no doubt in my mind that she would have disapproved strongly. After all, it was blackmail. But had he not considered his own danger and left for her somewhere, somehow, the identity of the man he was to meet last night?

Teresa made a sound like a chuckle. "Well, it would have had to be in Braille and Fernando could not write very well in Braille, although sometimes he would try."

"Well, if he did leave something for you, where would it be?"

Teresa's face lit up. "Can you hand me the third book from the right on the first shelf of the bookcase?"

I stood up and got the book she had asked for. It was thick with thick pages. Teresa opened the book to the middle and began moving her fingertips quickly over the pages. Sometimes she would pause at a particular place and let her fingertips move back and forth along the same spot. She seemed to check every page from the middle of the book to the end.

"No, there is nothing new here." Teresa closed the book and handed it back to me.

"Please think, Teresa, is there anything at all that he may have mentioned to you that would help us?"

"I'm sorry. There is nothing."

It occurred to me that there was a possibility that if Fernando had my name and number in his book then I may have been the person that he was going to tell, and, it may have been Fernando who had called my house that evening. The call that Penny had taken.

"Did he mention my name to you in any way, Teresa?"

"No, but…" Teresa paused and once again brushed her long hair back over one shoulder. "The only thing he said was, after he had read the article to me in the paper about the grocer, was that the investigation might lead the police down a strange path."

This was exactly the type of information that I was looking for. I was irritated that Teresa had not mentioned this before.

"Did you ask him what he meant by that, Teresa?"

"Are you angry with me?"

"No, of course not."

Teresa waited a moment or so. "Well I did ask him, but at that same time a man came to the door and they spoke outside for a while. I asked him who it was and he said it was a man placing a bet."

I scribbled a few more notes. "Teresa, who was it that came tonight to inform you about Fernando?"

"I missed his name. He spoke with a very raspy voice. I left to see the priest."

"Yes, that would be Officer Tee." I paused. "Teresa would you mind if I looked around in Fernando's room?"

"No, I would not mind."

I walked into a small bedroom that contained a bed, a chair, a small dresser, and a closet. I looked through the pockets of each of the slacks and coats. In the inside pocket of a gray corduroy jacket I found a slip of paper which contained my telephone number. To my way of thinking that confirmed my theory. I was to be Fernando's insurance. I was convinced that it was his call that Penny had taken. I figured that the best insurance for Fernando was to have the killer of Benavidez arrested for murder. What I could not figure out was why Fernando had picked me of all the cops on the force.

I moved to the dresser where there were two stacks of sporting magazines. I quickly rifled through them but found nothing. Inside the second drawer of the dresser there were several small notebooks similar to the one that we had found on the victim. The dates on the books were from the previous summer back to the previous year. I sat on the bed and scanned each one. I was wondering if perhaps one of those books might have a list somewhere that would have the names that corresponded to the numbers. I noticed that each of the numbers were of three digits except one which was the number 23 and it was by that number that a bet had been placed on the ninth of the previous May for fifteen hundred dollars on a horse by the name of *Sombra* at three to one odds. The bettor had apparently lost since there was no entry in the pay out column.

When I came back out of the bedroom, Teresa was sitting on the couch praying a rosary. "I think that Fernando was going to call you with the information of the man who killed the grocer." Teresa's voice was very soft.

"Yes, I think that too, Teresa." I sat down beside her. "Will you be okay?"

"Oh yes. I have an aunt across the river. She will come and stay with me or maybe I will go and live with her."

"Teresa, if there is anything that I can do for you I want you to call me."

"Well, I can't do that."

Thinking that she might have difficulty in using the dial on the telephone, I said, "Perhaps you can get a neighbor to dial for you."

"I can't do that either."

"Why not, Teresa?"

"Because you have not given me your number." She was teasing me. I gave her my number, which she repeated back to me. She held up her hand and tilted her head slightly toward the front of the house. "Someone is coming, Vince." After a moment or two there was a knock on the door. It was Pete. He said that Evan had sent him to take me back to the station. Before I left, Teresa once again ran her fingers across my hand.

— 19 —

Pete talked all the way to the station. He was still quite agitated and there were a couple of times when I thought he might yank the steering wheel off of the column. I remembered what Evan had said about the fact that whoever had called Pete and Torres had picked both of our ex-partners. Maybe it was just a coincidence but it was still strange. In other words, why would there be a need to call two different officers? I mentioned this to Pete. Pete grabbed the steering wheel hard again and said, "Did it occur to you guys that Torres might have been there on his own?" I looked over at Pete. I could see him clearly in the light of the dashboard. He had a hard cast to his face and his jaw muscles jutted out.

Torres was coming out of the station when Pete and I got there. He was walking very quickly and did not look our way. I was getting ready to get out of the car when I remembered that Penny had borrowed mine. Pete drove me on home and I arrived in time to have breakfast with Penny. I did not tell her everything that had happened, only mentioning what I deemed to be the highlights. I told Penny that Evan seemed to be at least considering the possibility that it may have been Benavidez' lover who had killed Obregon.

The newspaper had a short front-page article by Octavio Ochoa that said, without actually saying flat out, that Fernando Bingham Obregon had been killed as an act of revenge because he had been the killer of Solares, the grocer, whose real name was Faustino

Benavidez. Mr. Ochoa had a way with words and there was no doubt about it. The article said that Obregon had killed Benavidez to avenge his father's death back in the twenties in a place called Santa Rosa. I wondered if perhaps Evan had given this information to Octavio in exchange for keeping out the fact that my name and telephone number had been found on the victim. I was relieved at this omission but I was concerned about Teresa and how she would feel when she heard the news.

"That is not your take on this homicide is it Vin?" Penny handed me a plate with toast for me to butter.

"No, Penny."

"The victim, this Fernando Bingham Obregon, wouldn't be carrying around his disguise would he?"

"I find that hard to believe, Penny."

"It was planted on him?"

"Well, that is what I thought when I first saw him but then, later, after I talked to his sister, I began to think that he had brought it with him."

Penny frowned at me. "You say it was not his disguise but still he had it with him?"

"Yes." I buttered the toast slowly. Penny tapped her fingers on the table. I was not trying to build the suspense nor trying to put Penny off. I was merely trying to put all that had happened into a setting that made sense. I could see the color come up to Penny's cheeks. I smiled at her, which only served to bring up more color. She clenched her teeth. I went ahead quickly. "Suppose that the killer is running away from the grocery store and the veil is blown away by the wind and someone sees him? And suppose further that this person follows him and sees the killer of Benavidez discard the disguise and the gun?"

In an instant Penny spoke the word. "Blackmail!"

"Yes, Penny, I believe that Obregon saw the killer of Benavidez and that he was in the process of collecting the second payment of the blackmail amount." Penny looked at me. "The second payment, Vin?" I explained to Penny that Obregon had transferred an amount equal to five hundred dollars in gold to a bank in Parral, Mexico. Penny's eyes lit up. "So, you are saying that the killer tried to stall the blackmailer?"

"That seems reasonable to me, Penny."

"And the killer says to the blackmailer, bring me the disguise and the gun and then I will pay you the other half?" Penny thought for a moment. "Hmmm, yes, otherwise there would be no end to the blackmail."

I told Penny what Teresa had told me about her veil, that Obregon had taken it and bought her a new one. And that the veil that was in the satchel was not torn at all. Penny seemed to ponder this and then she said, "Yes, he would want the disguise to be complete. So, Obregon is on his way to get his second payment. He has with him the disguise in the satchel plus the gun and the deck of cards. He knows that he is dealing with a killer. Is the risk worth five hundred dollars? What is his insurance?" Penny was silent for a moment.

"Penny, I think that it would be worth the risk if he believed that with those thousand dollars he and his sister could move back to Parral and reopen their mother's bookstore." I looked at Penny, she nodded in agreement. I went on. "Penny, in Obregon's notebook there was a note on a separate piece of paper and on that paper was my name and our telephone number." Without hesitation Penny said, "He was the man who called last night?"

"Yes, I have no doubt. So, I need to know what he said. Did he sound excited, agitated?"

"No. He asked to speak to you. Sounded calm, polite. He spoke proper Spanish."

"His words, Penny?"

"He asked for you, may I please speak to Detective Quiñones. He is not here, I said. He was quiet for a moment so I said, as you have told me when you are not here, that he should leave a message or if necessary to call the station and speak to an officer there. It seems to me that he either coughed or chuckled when I said that. Then he thanked me and said that he would try later."

I was not hungry at all but I ate my toast and scrambled eggs anyway. "Vin, all of the others, including Benavidez, were shot but Obregon is stabbed. Like his father. Does that mean anything?"

"I am sure it does mean something, Penny. But what that is I have no idea." I had considered that detail just as I was sure that Evan had. It seemed that in the majority of crimes of passion a knife was used as opposed to a gun. I thought that that was why Evan had begun to suspect that it may have been Benavidez' lover who had killed Obregon. Sometimes, however, knives were used simply because of their silence.

"You do not have to go to the station this morning, do you?" Penny asked.

"No. Not till late afternoon. Evan wants us to meet in his office at four. Will you be getting your car back today?"

"Yes. Josie will come by and give me a ride to the garage. You need to get some sleep, Vin." Penny's eyes softened. "Promise me that you will be careful?"

I smiled at Penny. She knew that something was out of the ordinary.

After Penny left, I sat alone in the kitchen going over the entire case from the beginning. As far as the Club of Clubs was concerned, all the pieces were in place. The *bastos* and *carteros* were real. I believed that Octavio's article had set the events in motion. It was shortly after that, according to the record, that the three would-be victims had applied for citizenship. They figured that it would be a way to protect themselves. Benavidez must have gotten the idea about the playing cards from the article also and he had killed the others out of fear that they would turn on him. Neither *basto* nor *cartero* had killed Benavidez. No, he had been killed by someone else. I felt sure that Obregon had seen the killer and I felt sure that he had tried to blackmail him.

I sat and smoked a cigarette from Josie's leftover pack and thought out the situation. I allowed the thoughts of my theory to carry me wherever they would. The scenes began to play out in my mind.

Rosalinda is home on the day the linoleum is replaced. She sees the gold in the trunk. Later, she mentions this to Torres who is in a bad way financially. This is the answer to all of his problems. He figures out a plan. Maybe he tells Rosalinda that with that money they can start a new life somewhere together but there is no way that Rosalinda will agree to murder. Of this I was certain. So Torres' plan has to be of robbery only. On some night when both Benavidez and Benny are gone, Rosalinda lets Torres in and he takes the gold. But suppose Torres had figured out two plans? One that he tells Rosalinda and the other that he does not? So, Rosalinda lets Torres in and he takes the gold. Maybe there was just enough gold to pay off Torres' debt. Or maybe they just couldn't leave for one reason or another. Now, Rosalinda says to Torres, my uncle is going to know who took it. Don't worry, says Torres, I'll take care of it. Torres picks out a day and a disguise. Torres says to Rosalinda, you go to church every Sunday night, right? Yes, says Rosalinda. And your little brother usually spends week-ends at some friend's house, right? Yes, she answers. By the way, Torres says, does your uncle keep a pistol handy? Yes, on a shelf inside the counter. Okay, thinks Torres, I'll need to distract him for a second. I'll ask him for a pack of cigarettes. He'll turn slightly to get them. That's all I need. But Torres does not tell Rosalinda that. Instead, he tells her that he is going in right at closing and force Benavidez back into the storage room and tie him up and gag him. Then he will go into the kitchen and roll away the linoleum and take out the trunk and make it look like the gold is taken that night. Then he goes out the back and no one's the wiser. But then, something had gone wrong. He had been seen by someone, and that someone was Obregon. So, Obregon gets in touch with Torres. I saw you, he says, and I want a thousand dollars to keep quiet.

In the hands of any other person the disguise would mean nothing, but in the hands of the person who had seen the killer it was very valuable indeed. Torres had to find a way, and quickly, to get the articles back. Torres was smart, but still I wondered how he had lured Obregon for the second payment. But then again maybe it had not been difficult. The promise of another five hundred in gold might make a person a little less than cautious. And besides that, Obregon had my number. I believed that he believed that I was his insurance. I wondered if Torres had gotten a chuckle out of that. The police would find a dead man with the disguise of a killer in his bag and my name and telephone number in his pocket. It was perfect.

I made a list of all the items that had caused me to suspect Torres. Looking at them on paper I could see that for each instance there could be an easy rebuttal. The veil could have blown on to the oleander bush from just about anywhere. I had smelled the aftershave on Torres when he had brushed past me in Rosalinda's kitchen but there were probably a thousand men in El Paso in addition to Torres who used "Barrington's." Perhaps it had been

Torres' words instead of the sound of his voice that had agitated Benny. And, it could be merely a coincidence that Rosalinda had called me Detective Q, and so on and so on. So I had nothing really except the conviction that my hunch was absolutely right. I smoked another cigarette and then a plan started to form itself in my head. I thought it out. I would need help, I knew, and that is when I remembered Mona Reyes. I had noticed how Torres pursued her. I would not be able to tell her much, of course. I would have to frame my plan in such a way as to make it seem as though I was merely asking a favor on behalf of a friend. I showered and shaved quickly.

I drove to the Blue Moon hoping to catch Mona there. The place is a big, two-story brick building on Stanton Street. The bottom floor contains a dance floor and a restaurant and a bar. The second floor contains a large pool hall, private card game rooms, and another bar. On either side of the main entrance double doors are two very large plate glass windows. The windows are half circles. They have a tint to them so that at night, when the light from inside spills out to the sidewalk, it has a bluish glow. The Blue Moon never closes.

When I got there someone had already swept the snow away from the entrance. According to my watch, there should have been the light of dawn but the dark clouds allowed only the feeblest light to come through. There were two mounds of blue snow on either side of the doors. I went inside and asked one of the waitresses for Mona.

"Oh, tonight was her night off." She said, as she stuck her pencil back into her hair.

"Does she still live on Tays Street?" I asked.

"That's right, honey." The waitress said, as she walked off toward another table.

At 7:05 I knocked on Mona's door on Tays Street. It had gotten even darker than before, as though we were heading into dusk instead of dawn. After a few moments I heard Mona's voice. "Who is it?"

"Vince." I answered, thinking that I had made a foolish decision.

"Vince Quiñones?"

"Yes, Mona, I'm sorry to bother you. Maybe I should—"

"No, no." Mona said, as she opened her door. "Please, come in."

Mona was still quite young, maybe eighteen. She smiled. Her hair was in curlers of various colors. "Well, what a surprise." She said as she gestured for me to sit down. A small gas heater glowed in the corner of her tiny living room.

"I'm sorry, Mona." I said again. "But I have a favor to ask of you. Are you alone?"

She smiled broadly; she had a dazzling smile. "Yes, Vince, and sure, anything." She opened her eyes wide and raised her eyebrows at me. Even without make up she was still quite pretty.

"No, Mona, not along those lines." I smiled.

She repeated my exact words back to me. "No, Mona, not along those lines." She stretched out the word "those" in a low, husky way. Then she stuck out her lower lip in a fake pout. I laughed. Mona was certainly one of a kind.

"In that case, I should make us breakfast." She said. "But first let me do this." She sat down next to me and crossed her legs and began to unclip her curlers. Her shiny, black, healthy-looking hair sprang up as she did this and then it unraveled down in long spirals. She placed the curlers in neat rows on the table next to the couch. "Please," she said, "come into the kitchen." I told Mona that I had already had breakfast, to which she smirked at me and said, "I'll just bet."

As Mona busied herself with making coffee and breakfast, I thought of the circumstances under which I had first met her.

On a very hot day in July, during the time that I had been a uniformed officer, and Pete and I were making our rounds of our sector, a woman came running down the street toward us.

"Please hurry," she screamed at us, "there's a man about to kill a young girl at Tays and Seventh."

When Pete and I arrived on the scene there was a man holding a machete to the throat of a pretty young girl, who looked to be about fourteen or fifteen years old. They were standing in the middle of the intersection while the crowd pleaded with him to let her go. The man was yelling that he would kill her if anyone got close. He kept wiping at his brow with a handkerchief. She began yelling also when she saw us. It seemed to me that the man had let a squabble get out of hand because there was no conviction in his words. He was looking for a way out. I drew my gun and started walking slowly toward them, speaking calmly. Pete, approaching them from the rear, called out, "If you hurt that girl we are not going to kill you. No, we will not kill you. What we will do is shoot your balls off and then send you to prison. Do you know what we're saying here, *vatito*?"

Pete had not invented those words. It was a story he and I had heard from an old cop in the locker room. Startled, the man started to turn toward Pete and as he did so he released his grip on the girl just enough for her to slip under his grasp and run over to me. She ran behind me and put her arms around me and began screaming curses, quite expertly, at the man. The man dropped the machete and raised his hands over his head.

The next day, Mona came by the station to see me. She said that I had saved her life, and told me that if there was ever anything I might need to call on her. She told me that she had been on her own since age thirteen and that the man who had threatened her was her "manager." She said that she was leaving that business to earn an honest living. I had seen her now and then afterward, usually at the Blue Moon where she worked as a waitress. She always repeated her offer to me.

"Are you working tonight, Mona?" I asked.

"Yes." She said. "What did you have in mind?"

Mona set a nice table. We chatted easily together, speaking of many things. I began to eat out of politeness. Mona made strong coffee and a very good breakfast.

— 21 —

I drove back home and tried to get some sleep. I was dreaming a strange dream when the telephone rang.

"Hello, Vincent?"

"Yes, Teresa." I recognized her voice right off. "Is something wrong?" I thought that she was calling me to complain about the allegation in the paper regarding her brother.

"No, nothing wrong. You asked me to call if there was anything I needed."

"Yes."

"Well, could you ask the police to quit coming around here?"

"What do you mean, Teresa?"

"Well, a Detective Torres came by a while ago."

My heart skipped a beat and I sat up quickly. "Torres?"

"Yes, he asked me the same questions that you did."

"Teresa, are you alone?" My concern for Teresa's safety caused my hands to tremble.

"Oh, no. My aunt and uncle are here with me." I heard Teresa answer a woman's question over the phone.

I relaxed. "Okay, that's good."

"Vincent?"

"Yes?"

"Is Torres from here?"

"Do you mean from South El Paso?"

"Yes."

"Yes, he is. Why?"

"His voice, his words. He slips so easily into slang."

"Yes, I suppose he does." I quickly thought of how I could ask Teresa if she had picked up something from the sound of Torres' voice. Perhaps a "shadow" as she had mentioned to me. Before I could phrase my question, Teresa spoke again. "Vince, I got the impression that Detective Torres knew who...that is, something about who may have done this to my brother." I thought to myself, *I'm sure he does,* but I did not say this. Teresa spoke again. "Vince, he wanted to know who it was that had come by to inform me about Fernando."

"Yes?"

"I told him that you had said that it was Officer Tee. Is that right?"

"Yes, that is correct." I paused. "What else did Detective Torres say?"

"He wanted to know if I had been interviewed by Officer Tee."

"Were you?"

"No, he just came by and informed me and then left, saying someone would come by later, which turned out to be you." Teresa cleared her throat. "Detective Torres was very interested in you."

"I see."

"Then he asked me to repeat to him all of your questions and my answers. Is that appropriate, Vincent?"

I hesitated. Usually, this was not out of the ordinary. But if Torres was trying to find out what I knew, that could be significant. This caused my stomach to flip around. "Well, yes, Teresa. You know police work is sometimes pretty repetitious. Did you tell him everything that you told me?"

"Yes, I guess. Some things he wrote down and some he didn't, just like you." Teresa paused. "He also went into Fernando's room, but he did not ask if he could the way you did."

"Well, I'm sorry about that, Teresa. He didn't take anything did he?"

"No, but he did ask me if Fernando knew you. He, like you, also said that there was a note in one of Fernando's jackets with your name and number. He asked me that question three times."

"Anything else, Teresa?"

"Yes, like you, he asked me if the number '23' had any meaning for me."

"You told me it did not, Teresa."

"That's right, it doesn't." Teresa paused, and then spoke again to her aunt, I assumed, then back to me. "Vince, Detective Torres has changing moods, doesn't he?"

"What do you mean, Teresa?"

"Well, when he got here he was like in a big hurry and spoke hard to me but later his voice softened so that it was like two different people." I was wondering what this could mean when Teresa spoke again. "Vince, my aunt says that Detective Torres is a very handsome man. Is he?"

"Well, Teresa, I guess." I really didn't know what to say to that question.

"Yes, she says that Detective Torres is as handsome as the Devil."

— 22 —

After Teresa and I said goodbye I tried to go back to sleep. It was no use. I could not stop my mind from racing. Still, I tried to sleep but after what seemed an hour I got up and took a long drive out on the highway. I was halfway to Las Cruces when I turned around and headed back to the city. I arrived at the station at four o'clock and walked directly to Evan's office. He was sitting at his desk with some crime scene photographs spread out before him.

"Good afternoon, Vinny. Did you get enough rest?"

"Good afternoon, Evan. Yes," I lied, since I hadn't gotten much rest at all, "how about you?"

"Could have been better." Evan continued to look at the photographs and did not look up at me. "I hear that Obregon has a sister. How did it go?"

I told Evan about Teresa, that she was blind and that Obregon had taken a black veil from her and that he had a receipt for five hundred dollars in gold. I paused for a moment or two. "She also told me that her brother had said that this investigation might take us down a strange path."

Evan looked up from the photographs and then looked back down at them. There were four photographs on Evan's desk. Each photograph had been taken from behind the body of the victim. The first three victims had been shot sitting at their kitchen tables. This I knew. What I had not known, nor had the newspapers ever been told, was that the playing cards had been folded in half. Not crosswise, as one might expect, but lengthwise. In each photograph the cards were standing up, facing the victim. Next to the photographs there were two sheets of paper with a list of names on each sheet.

Evan spoke. "Octavio had some interesting information for me last night." He leaned back slightly in his chair. "He says that some of the things he was able to discover pointed to the possibility that our victim last night was the son of the person who wrote the book about which Octavio spoke in his article." Evan lit a cigarette. "What this would add up to, Vin, is that the woman who I saw push Benavidez off of that cliff back then was the writer of 'The Club of Clubs' and also that she was the mother of Obregon and that Jacob Bingham was his father." Evan looked away, out of the window.

"Evan, Teresa did not mention the book. Maybe she didn't know about it but she did say that her mother said that Obregon's father was killed in Santa Rosa."

Evan looked at me. What he and I were talking about was a motive for murder if ever there was one. The only thing wrong with that conclusion was that Teresa's mother had always believed that she had pushed Benavidez to his death. Teresa believed this and there was no reason to believe that Fernando thought otherwise. I spoke. "Evan, I don't think that Obregon killed Benavidez."

"No, Vin, neither do I." Evan sat forward again. "I must admit that I was not quite myself night before last, Vinny. But last evening, as I was describing how Jacob had folded his card, it struck me about the way these cards had been folded. We know that Benavidez folded the first three cards. Then, he is murdered. Now, who would know to fold the last card in that same way?"

My heart began to race. "I would say, Evan, that it would have to be someone close to the investigation." As I was speaking, the telephone rang. Evan picked it up. "Yes, Billings? Go ahead." Billings was one of our dispatchers, and as he spoke Evan made notations next to each name on one of the sheets. They appeared to be times and locations.

"All right. Thanks." Evan said and hung up. "I'm sorry, Vinny, you said someone close to the investigation?"

I did not tell Evan how I had arrived at my conviction, only that I had a strong hunch as to the killer. I simply told Evan that what I needed was for he and I and Rosalinda to drive by the Blue Moon at 10:30 that night. Evan looked at me for a long moment. Then he studied the list of names. "You feel strongly about this, Vinny?"

"Very strongly." I said.

Evan rubbed his eyes slowly, moving his thumb and index finger toward the bridge of his nose. He continued this motion for what seemed a long time. My throat began to tighten. Evan handed me the two sheets of paper. On the first sheet were the names of all of the individuals who had access to the 1950 crime scenes. Some of the names had been crossed out. On the second sheet were the remaining names. Next to each of those names was noted the time between 9:30 and 10:30 on Sunday night prior and the location from which the individual had checked in. By some of the names was the entry: "Off duty."

Evan looked at me. "The person you suspect, his name is there?"

"Yes." I answered. My voice sounded strange to me.

Evan stood up and walked to the window. He stood there looking out at the last rays of the setting sun for several minutes. It was very quiet; the only sound was the clock ticking on the wall. With his back to me he spoke, his voice suddenly quite hoarse. "Who do you think it is, Vin?"

I had come this far. I would not equivocate. "Torres."

Still with his back to me, Evan looked out of the window for another long while. I thought that perhaps he had not heard me. Then he began speaking.

"Serial killers put a particular strain on law enforcement, Vin. We are paid to protect and then..." Evan became silent again. I looked at the shadows moving along the wall. Evan started again. "I think that Tommy changed during the time of the second and third murders, or maybe he had begun to change even before that. I don't know. And I don't know what caused it, but he began to take it personally, began to think that it was a matter of winning and losing, and he couldn't bear to lose. That, Vinny, is something a detective should never do because that will wear you down and out before your time. You can only do what you can do. Sometimes you are lucky, sometimes not. You move on, and believe in tomorrow."

Evan stopped talking. He continued looking out the window. In a low voice he said, "However, Vincent, Tommy is a good man, and a good detective. A very good detective..." Evan did not finish. I waited. "When you work side by side with someone in this business you become very close. More like brothers, actually." Evan turned to face me. There was sadness in his voice. "Your hunch is strong, Vinny?"

"Yes."

"I must tell you, I hope to God that you are wrong."

"I'm sorry, Evan." I said, and truly meant it

— 23 —

At 10:15 Evan and Rosalinda came out of the holding center. The night was clear and cold. I was waiting on the driver's side of the back seat of Evan's car. Evan opened the back door, on the passenger side, and Rosalinda slid in beside me. She looked no better now than the last time I had seen her. To me, the strain of her involvement in the matter was evident upon her face. Some suspects cannot hold the lie within them for long. Evan had told her that we needed her assistance in reevaluating the crime scene.

"How's Benny?" I asked her as Evan started up the car.

Rosalinda looked at me. She did not answer me right away. As we drove out of the parking lot, she said, "He is fine." Her words were a mere whisper.

We drove down Stanton Street toward the Blue Moon. The snow had melted during the day. There were puddles of water, starting to freeze up, all along the street. I could feel the crunch of the ice on the tires as we passed over them. My heart was skipping beats. I did not feel confident at all about the whole matter. I forced myself to breathe slowly.

During my drive that afternoon I had stopped and walked out into the desert to be alone with my thoughts. As I walked among the snow-dusted mesquite and cacti, a realization had come to me. The seriousness of the situation struck me hard. I was involved in a great gamble of my own making, and I didn't know which was worse, for my hunch to be right or for it to be wrong. One thing was certain, whichever way this came out it would be bad. If my hunch was right, Torres would go to prison convicted of first degree murder. There could be no doubt about that. But what if I was wrong? What then? I would look like a fool for one thing and the second thing was that I might find it necessary to resign on the spot. I kept telling myself that it was not too late to back out.

Now, as we moved slowly down the street, everything took on a vividness that I could not explain. Everything was too sharply defined. The pools of light beneath the streetlights looked as though they had been painted there. The usual soft diffusion of light as it fades into shadow was missing. There was light and then there was blackness, with nothing in between. The world looked strange as it slipped by. I had the feeling that we were traveling sideways, like a long slow slide on ice. Up ahead, the Blue Moon loomed as large as a ship in the bay.

I was counting on Rosalinda's temper. I had asked Mona to call Torres and tell him that she had some information for him. She was to seat him at the table closest to the window and at exactly 10:30 she was to be sitting on his lap and then kiss him as we drove by. If what I believed was true, Rosalinda would react strongly to that scene. It was at that moment, when her anger overtook her, that I had planned to say to her that I knew everything. I felt that at that moment she would blurt out the truth. Now, as we moved slowly down the street I was not sure about anything.

As we drove by the Blue Moon, Mona was standing at the window. When she saw us, she spread her arms in a gesture like a question or frustration. I could not see Torres. My plan had failed. I felt sick. Evan continued past the restaurant and down to the next block. He waited for the streetcar to move by us. It moved very slowly. The streetcar was empty except for one gray-haired woman who was sitting very erect with a worried look on her face. She looked out directly at me and then she seemed to shake her head. I saw her pass a thin hand across her face. Evan made a U-turn and drove slowly back up to the establishment. It was 10:30 exactly. In the light at the side of the restaurant, in the narrow alley, I saw Torres' car. *Why is he not inside?*

"Why...?" Rosalinda began to speak. Then she turned and looked into the restaurant. Mona once again made her outstretched hands gesture. Evan pulled over and then he turned back to look at me with raised eyebrows. Now I could see clearly that Torres was sitting in his car with his head tilted back. "I'm sorry, Evan." I managed to say. Evan did not respond to me. He got out and walked over to Torres' car.

"Why are we stopping here?" Rosalinda asked, as she sat straight up. I saw Evan looking into the window of Torres' car and then he jumped back, as though he had been shocked by some electrical current. He put his hand up to his face and then he slumped with his back against the side of the car. Slowly, he motioned for me to come over. My knees were shaking as I approached. I looked into the open window at Torres. There was a trickle of blood down his left cheek. He had been shot in the temple. Torres was dead.

— 24 —

A month has passed, and although the memory of that night is very clear I try not to think about it. In spite of my efforts, not a day has gone by that at least for a few minutes I have wallowed in the muddy pit of regret, self-pity, and self-doubt. It is at those moments that I am stricken by the painful realization of the fact that while I was looking at Torres as a suspect, he was on the trail of the real killer. It is a realization that descends upon me with the force of a baseball bat on the top of my head.

Two things happened that night which are especially clear. One was the look of absolute terror on Rosalinda's face as I drove her back to the holding center. The other thing was later when I returned to the crime scene and Evan and I sat in his car. I had offered to resign but he would not hear of it. He said that the department needed me now more than ever. He also told me that a homicide detective without the balls to gamble on his hunches was in the wrong business. All the while, as Evan spoke, I kept looking over at Torres' car as an overwhelming sense of fatigue came over me. I did not have the strength to turn away. Evan spoke to me for a long time, and he never mentioned to anyone else that I had suspected Torres. I told Evan about my plan, that I had gotten Mona to call Torres to come and see her there at the restaurant. What this boiled down to was that it had been me who had lured Torres to his death. There was no way around it. Evan had left me in the car and walked into the Blue Moon and talked to Mona himself. She, as far as I knew, had never mentioned this to anyone else either.

All of this didn't seem to matter in the end because if at the time of the murder of Obregon my name had not appeared in the newspapers, after the murder of Torres it did. The newspapers began to mention two facts which taken together had a chilling effect. They began to say that my name had been found in a notebook on the body of a known gambler and that whoever had killed Tommy Torres had taken his notebook from him. This was true. It was evident to all of us that not only was Torres very close to finding the killer of Benavidez and Obregon but may have known exactly who he was. I began to receive so many calls at home that I had to have my number changed.

I went alone to Torres' wake. I did not ask Penny to go with me. I sat in the back of the church and watched as dozens of people went by. Evan and Bellamy came and sat with me for a while and then they left. I waited until the church was empty and then I walked up to the open coffin. I stood there wanting to speak but nothing came out. Torres was wearing a hat, which they had tilted slightly to cover the wound on his left temple. In the flickering candlelight I saw Torres' lips move and then as clear as anything I heard his voice. *You were wrong about me. The real killer is out there. Catch him!* I walked out of the church and headed for the nearest bar and stayed there until it closed. I was not able to get drunk, and not a single ounce of my pain was relieved.

My life has slipped into a world of paper. As a result of the murder of Torres, and the massive investigation that sprang to life, a new position was created in the police department. The title was Chief of Detectives and the job was given to Evan. One of his first acts in this new capacity was to name me as the coordinator of all investigations regarding the deaths of Benavidez, Obregon, and Torres. It was a very large project indeed. I was given the authority to interview anyone, including any person in the police department. This included access to all personnel files. I was told that I was to write a report with every single relevant detail of all the homicides including the three murders committed by Benavidez in 1950. Sometimes I wonder if all of this was to get both Evan and I off of the streets. I don't know, but I threw myself into my new job. I immersed myself in it fully, totally, and completely. One of the first things I did was to borrow the book from Octavio. I read it twice. I tended to agree with Octavio that it had been written by a woman except for the graphic descriptions of the battle scenes in the fight for control of Chihuahua. I found it difficult to believe that a woman could describe such scenes with such power. There is a battle scene in which the writer speaks of a human ear landing on the barrel of his (or her) rifle and how the writer removes it and scratches a small hole into the hard earth and buries it and then begins firing again. I also agreed with Octavio that the plot of the book was as complex as the game of chess although the pieces here were living, breathing humans. In the end, I found the book useful in establishing a foundation for the thought processes that went into the making of a person hell-bent on revenge. Their sole purpose in life was to end the life of another. I moved from the book to the cases at hand and became engulfed in the mounds photographs, interviews, and boxes of evidence. Then, one day, Penny asked me if I thought that it would better if she left.

"Leave?" I asked. "Why?"

Penny looked away. "Well, you don't seem to need me around anymore. You're gone eighteen hours a day and when you're here you never have anything to say to me."

She was right. In the past month I had been completely engrossed in my own misery and my own pursuits. She had tried to engage me in conversations about my project but I had only grunted a short reply here and there. In the deep fog of my life I had not noticed the depth of her feelings. The thought of Penny turning her back on me was more than I could bear. It was that sinking feeling that made me jump out of my chair and rush to embrace her. I don't even know what all I said to her or whether I made any sense but she began to relax in my arms and embraced me back.

I knew then that it was time to tell her about my misguided theory. I led her to the kitchen and we sat down and I told her everything. It hurt me to tell her how very wrong I had been but in the end she placed her smooth, flawless, hand on mine and said, "I'm sorry to have been such a crybaby, Vin. I didn't know."

"I am sorry too, Penny. But I must do this. I am going to get this guy or die trying."

Penny took my hand in both of hers and squeezed tight. "Please do not use that term, Vin."

25

The paperwork that is waiting on my desk every morning is so immense that I have been given an assistant. He is a rookie who has been on the street for about a year. His name is Rudy Tarang. He is full of energy and enthusiasm. He told me that he had wanted to be a policeman since he was six years old. I don't know why that fact makes me wonder about him. Can he be serious about that? When I was informed that I would be getting him, I went down and pulled his personnel file. It showed that he was from South El Paso and had graduated from Bowie High. His folder said that he could type eighty-five words a minute and knew shorthand. Rudy had been in one of Penny's classes. She told me that he was quite bright but rather casual about homework and school in general. Penny also told me that he was the type of young man who had a hard time keeping profanity out of his vocabulary. It seemed to me that Rudy was more impressed with the fact that I was Penny's husband than the fact that I was a detective and that for all intents and purposes I was his boss.

"Mrs. Quiñones is your wife?" His eyebrows shot up.

"Yes."

Rudy studied me up and down, seemingly sizing me up. "She is the best damn teacher in the whole high school."

"I am glad to hear you say that, Rudy. Now, let's get to work."

"Damn right. Let's catch that sonofabitch." Rudy made me laugh.

That evening I told Penny what Rudy had said and she laughed also. "That sounds like Rudy. What is it that he does for you, anyway?"

"I have begun with the three murders in 1950. We are pulling all the old files and compiling all of the interviews at that time. There are to be three cross-referenced books. One contains the coroner's reports plus all forensics findings, the second includes all of the crime scene photographs, and the third contains the actual interviews. These, I am to whittle down to the bare bones of the conversation between officer and witness. Rudy is an excellent typist. I take a file, jot down only the most relevant facts, and then I give it to Rudy for him to type. I am trying to get all of the interrogations down in an outline form and then pick out the details, which point to a pattern. In addition, at the end of any particular interview, I am adding a personal history of each of the interviewers."

Penny's eyes lit up. "So, that is the real purpose?"

Penny sensed this on her own. I had not told her that Evan himself had suspected that someone close to the investigations of the three murders in 1950 had been the murderer of Benavidez. That is, someone who had known how the playing cards had been folded. It was this fact that allowed me to keep my head above water. But barely. "Yes, and no, Penny. I do not intend to focus in one direction or another." I began to slip away to the night at the Blue Moon when Penny nudged me back. "Yes, Vin, go on."

"Right. This will be for Evan and the Chief to decide. No one else is to read my report. It will be for internal purposes only. Also, as a precaution and as a matter of confidentiality, the police officers and all other individuals involved in the investigations of the crimes are identified by number, not by name. Evan created the list of random numbers."

"But you know who they are."

"Yes, I take the files and associate the name of the police officer to Evan's list and thereafter the officer is identified by number only."

"Including yourself?"

"Yes, Evan and I and the Chief all have numbers."

"These secret numbers. You cannot tell me?"

"No."

Penny placed both hands on the table. She spoke in a voice like Marlene Dietrich. "We have ways of making you talk, you know. Yes, very effective ways of making you talk." I laughed. We both stood up at the same time and went into the bedroom.

— 26 —

Rudy and I have completed the first part of our task. We have reduced the files of the first three murders to just over one hundred typed pages. As an introduction to that segment I have quoted from Octavio Ochoa's article in the newspaper that he in turn correctly attributed to the book, "The Club of Clubs." As I had originally thought, it was the publishing of Octavio's article that had started things in motion, or at least provided Benavidez with a plan for casting suspicion toward revenge as a motive. At the end of that segment, on a single page, is a list of numbers corresponding to the three homicides of 1950. In the case of the first homicide, there are only nine numbers. These are the numbers signifying the individuals who had the opportunity to see the folded card at the crime scene. The numbers go from the first officer, or officers, to arrive at the crime scene on down to the crime scene photographer. This is the list of all individuals who were in and about the crime scene itself and who may have seen the folded playing card. These numbers include Evan's and Torres' numbers. The numbers are further refined so as to exclude any individual, by virtue of time cards and dispatcher records, and other corroborating information, whose physical location on the night of November fifth would have made it impossible to be close enough to the Benavidez crime scene to actually do it. It is a strange thing for me to be establishing alibis for fellow cops but that is what it has boiled down to. The total number for all of the 1950 homicides after the exclusions is twenty-two. I have memorized the names that correspond with the numbers. They are with me all the time. Some of these individuals I know quite well, others not at all except by name. I have kept in mind Bellamy's words about Rosalinda having a lover and, for my own purposes, I have further whittled down the list of twenty-two down to nine. These are men who are no older than forty. I do not believe that Rosalinda would date any man older than that.

We have issued orders, at Evan's insistence, that each of the individuals who were the first civilians to discover the bodies in 1950 be re-interviewed. We were aware that a small number of people other than law enforcement had seen the playing cards and the manner in which they were folded. On the other hand, I recalled that back then there had been a few instances, which were not Club murders, where a victim's relative insisted that he or she had seen a playing card at the scene where no such thing existed. Such is the power of murder.

We are now working the Benavidez homicide, which is more difficult to trim down because it is still open. I had left my shorthand notes, the ones I had taken when Evan had questioned Rosalinda, intact and then followed them up with the transcription to standard writing later in my notebook. I found myself lingering over these notes and the rest of them and mulling over the sequence of events that led me so incorrectly to Torres. I lingered over them too long apparently because Evan, who checks on us every day, told me that I should give my notes to Rudy and let him determine how we are to use them in the second part of our book. It seemed to me that Rudy's chest puffed out about six inches when Evan gave him this new chore.

In the past two weeks Rudy has grown increasingly more casual with me. Sometimes I get the feeling that he is not very impressed with me. I think that he thinks that I am entirely too slow for him.

I cannot put my finger on it exactly but it seems to me that Rudy thinks that he can solve this crime on his own. As though he senses that we are now into a new territory and it is here where he will find our answer. I have found out one thing about Rudy. If in high school he was casual about homework, as Penny had said, it was probably because he was bored with it. He is actually quite bright and he handles my notebooks with great care, almost like some sacred object, which makes me smile. Then he buries his head into those small books as though he is reading the most interesting novel. I keep my eyes on him. I know that he has read them more than once.

I am working with Evan's notes, and I suppose that I am as interested in them as Rudy is in mine. What I noticed first of all about Evan's notes was that they are very neat and concise except for one point. When he had made his entry for the time, date, and address at the grocery store his hand is steady. The next few entries are quite shaky and then his notes regarding Rosalinda are once again quite neat. My assumption was that after Evan recognized Benavidez, he had become unnerved and under the circumstances I could understand why. After all, this was the man who very probably had killed his father. But, these were exactly the types of things that we were looking for. The smallest detail out of the ordinary. It was these types of variances that we would add to the individuals' history at the end. I had to address the issue. As I was making a note to confirm this with Evan, Rudy spoke. "Hey, Vince, your notes, when you arrive at the grocery store your notes are neat. Then, when you go inside they get a little shaky for a while then neat again. What's the deal?"

I laughed. I had not noticed this myself. Rudy was looking straight into my eyes. He was serious about all of this. "Rudy, if my notes appear different to you it is because I was interviewing a person that I knew."

I waited for Rudy to ask me how well I knew this person to cause a noticeable change in my writing. We looked at each other for a few moments. It seemed to me that a look of surprise and then understanding came into his eyes. Rudy looked down into my notes and then back up at me. "So, should I put this in your history?"

"Yes, Rudy. You may say in my history that I knew her briefly."

"Right, sure Vince." But his eyes said *well, just how briefly?* Rudy went back to my notes. He read for a while and then looked back up again. "You know, Vince, I think that someone should re-interview this Rosalinda Lucero."

"Why do you think that, Rudy?"

"Because I think that she knows the killer."

I was amazed that Rudy could pick that up from my notes. I had made it a point to not make any notation regarding my suspicions. Indeed, at that point I had not yet developed any suspicion. I thought for a moment. "You get that from my notes?"

"I do."

"How?"

"Well, your notes are pretty straightforward. But then, when Evan tells Rosalinda Lucero that he is afraid that the person who killed her uncle may return to the store, you describe her movements very clearly." Rudy read from my notes. "Evan told Miss Lucero that the man who did this might come back to do her or Benny some harm. Miss Lucero immediately jumped from her chair and held her brother tightly, and cried into his hair." Rudy looked up at me, a quizzical look on his face, waiting.

"I don't know how you get anything from that, Rudy."

Rudy read my next line. "She would never do anything to hurt her brother."

I looked at Rudy. He was looking straight into my eyes. My first impulse was to tell young Rudy that there is nothing quite so aggravating as to have someone read your own words back to you and arrive at some conclusion far from your intentions. But that would be untrue. I knew what Rudy was getting at. And in spite of the fact that I had been completely wrong about Torres, still the trail led right back again to Rosalinda. There was no escaping it. But it was a path that made me very uncomfortable.

Rudy continued to look at me, waiting for me to speak. When I said nothing, he put my notebook down and said, "Do you want to know what I think, Vince?" I did not respond but merely made a gesture with my hand for him to go ahead.

"Well, okay. This Rosalinda gets to the store that night and sees her dead uncle and the card, right?"

"Yes, Rudy."

"Right. So at that time she should know that it is a Club murder, right?"

I looked at Rudy's enthusiastic face. "Assuming that she had read the papers back at the time of the others, yes, Rudy."

"Well, sure she did. Everybody did. So, she sees the card." Rudy looked at me, expectantly.

"Rudy," I spoke slowly, "there were those who didn't even see—"

Rudy did not wait for me to finish. "Don't you see, Vince? In all of the other murders the victims themselves had been the only target. Not any other member of the family. So, why does she react that way?"

I knew what Rudy was getting at. In none of the other murders in 1950 had any other member of the victims' families been harmed or even threatened. In each case, killer and victim had been alone. Back then, the evidence showed, the killer had shot the victims while sitting across from them at the victims' kitchen tables. I knew why Evan had said this to Rosalinda that night at the store. It was to get her and Benny out of the house so that we could look for the trunk, which based on his prior knowledge he reasoned had to be there. Now, I said. "You tell me, Rudy."

"Because she knows that this one is not a Club murder. This is something else. She knows the murderer, and something has gone very wrong."

I had the urge to walk over to Rudy and snatch my notebook from his hand. I wanted to see my notes again with my own eyes to see where Rudy was getting such ridiculous ideas. I had the urge to tell young Rudy that he had absolutely no future whatsoever in detective work. Instead, I sat there and said nothing but simply stared hard into Rudy's eyes until he looked away. We worked in silence for a few minutes and then, without looking up from my notebook, Rudy said, "You have written that Bellamy said that Rosalinda had a lover. Your hand is shaky again here."

I felt the blood rush to my neck. My voice was hard. "Damn it, Rudy, is there something you want to say here?"

Rudy's voice was soft. "No, Vince."

"Because if there is, you better go ahead and say it right here and now."

"Come on, Vince, these are things that we are supposed to be looking for."

"I don't give a damn what we are looking for. You either spit out what you're getting at or go on back to the street." As soon as I said those words I regretted them. I stood up and walked over to the window and looked out. I spoke without looking back at Rudy. "Hell, Rudy. I'm sorry. You've been a big help to me. You're right. These are exactly the kinds of things that we are looking for." I turned to look at Rudy. His eyes were wide. I smiled at him. His smile was brief, tentative. "Do you know Rosalinda, Rudy?"

"No, I don't."

"Then I think that you should be the one to interview her." I thought Rudy would be taken aback by my suggestion. But he was not. He jumped from his chair and said he was ready to go.

"Hold on, Rudy. We must approach this carefully."

I had not seen Rosalinda since the night I took her back to the holding center. On the day after Torres was killed, Rosalinda and Benny were released from the holding center and taken back to the tenement. Rosalinda quit her job as a translator and was running the store. I had driven by the tenement a couple of times in the hopes of seeing Benny but I had not seen him. As I was thinking about this, Evan walked in. "Vince, Miss Lucero is in my office. She wants to give a statement. I want you and Rudy there."

— 27 —

Rosalinda was sitting in front of Evan's desk. She had her hair tied up in a bun. I was surprised at how much weight she had lost. She was wearing a green sweater and a tan-colored skirt, and her sweater seemed to droop from her thin shoulders. "Miss Lucero, you know Detective Quiñones. This is his assistant, Officer Tarang." As Rosalinda turned to acknowledge Rudy, her eyes swept past mine and then back again to look at me for just a fraction of a second. She did not speak to either of us. I sat in a chair to the side of Evan at his desk. There was only one other chair in the back of the room to which Evan directed Rudy.

Evan spoke. "Officer Tarang, I would like you to document a full and complete record of what is said here this afternoon." I saw Rosalinda look quickly at Evan. Then Evan added, "Unless I direct you to do otherwise."

"Yes sir." Rudy flipped open his legal-size yellow notebook.

Evan began. "Miss Lucero is here of her own free will. No one has requested nor suggested her presence."

Rosalinda began to speak. In spite of her thin appearance, her voice sounded sure and strong, deep and husky. "I would like to say that some of the things that I have done are bad. Very bad. And I am very sorry for them, and ashamed. You, Detective Morrow, have said that you would treat me fairly. I speak freely this afternoon trusting in your word." Instinctively, I reached for my notebook, but with a gesture Evan made me put it back in my pocket.

Rosalinda went on. "On the twentieth of October of this year I was home from work when the linoleum was replaced in our kitchen. There was a trunk beneath the floorboard. There were bags of gold coin inside. My uncle opened one of them and said to me, 'when I die, this will be yours'. I had never known that he had that trunk buried there. I asked him where he had gotten it from and he told me that he had brought it with him from Mexico but that I should never mention this to anyone." Rosalinda paused and removed a small, white handkerchief from her purse. She dabbed at her eyes. Evan asked. "How much gold was there, Miss Lucero?" Rosalinda took a deep breath, "At the time I did not know, but later I found out there was seventeen thousand dollars in gold." Once again Rosalinda reached into her purse and removed a folded sheet of paper. She placed it on the table and slid it toward Evan. Evan opened it and read it quickly and then passed it to me. As I was reading it, Evan spoke to Rudy. "Let the record show that the victim, Benavidez, also known as Maximo Solares, executed a notarized last will and testament bequeathing all his possessions to Rosalinda Lucero."

Rosalinda cleared her throat and went on. "I had been dating..." Rosalinda paused and then looked down for a second. When she looked back up, she was looking directly into my eyes. "I had been dating Detective Torres for a few months and I told him about the gold." My hand moved up to loosen my tie, seemingly of its own accord. My mouth was suddenly dry.

"He had lost quite a bit of money gambling on the horses across the bridge. He told me that the people from across the bridge were getting impatient. He said that we could take the money, that he could pay off his debt and that we could run away together." A sob came up to Rosalinda's mouth, which she covered with her handkerchief. We all waited. She began speaking again, but softly. "On the Thursday before the night that my uncle was killed, when he was across the bridge and my brother, Benito, was asleep, I let Tommy into the house and he took the gold. I thought that we would be leaving for California the next day but he said that he needed a week or so to get everything ready. I told him that there was the danger that my uncle would look at his trunk again and that if he did he would know that it was me who had taken the gold." Rosalinda stopped talking, and asked Evan for a drink of water. As Evan stood up to get her a glass of water, I tried to catch her eyes again but she looked straight ahead. Her hand shook as she raised the glass of water to her mouth. "Torres said that there was a way to fix this. He said that he could go into the store at closing on a Sunday night. I usually go to church on Sunday nights and Benito spends the night at his friend's house on Florence. Benito was not supposed to be there." Rosalinda paused as a visible shudder ran through her body. "Torres told me that he was going to go in, force my uncle back to his room, gag him and tie him up. He told me that he would then go into the kitchen and fold back the linoleum and take the trunk out and leave it open. It would look like a robbery. I was to get back from church and untie uncle and tell him that I had seen a woman running down the street." Rosalinda took another drink of water and seemed to have difficulty in swallowing it. "Detective Morrow, I swear to you that this was the plan as it was told to me. I would not have agreed to the murder of my uncle, may he rest in peace."

I looked at Evan as Rosalinda spoke those words. I could not quite read the expression on his face. I saw that Evan held Rosalinda's eyes for a moment, and then he said, "I believe you

Miss Lucero." At these words from Evan, large tears sprang up to Rosalinda's eyes. "Please," Evan said, "go on."

Rosalinda, with her head down and with her handkerchief covering her eyes, spoke. "I asked him why he had done it. Why had he changed the plan? He told me he had done it that way, with the card and all, so that it would look like the other murders. But why? I asked him, but he wouldn't say."

I once again looked at Evan and wondered what he was thinking. It was clear to me that Torres would have hoped that a new Club murder would have assured his teaming up with Evan again. This thought had played a part in my own suspicions. Evan ran his hand through his hair and then he took out his pack of cigarettes and offered one to Rosalinda. I did not know that she smoked but she took it. Evan reached across the desk and lit it for her then he lit his own and slid the pack and the lighter over to me. I looked over at Rudy but he shook his head. I watched Rosalinda inhale deeply and then I lit my cigarette. The three of us sat for a few seconds in silence, smoking.

Rosalinda began speaking again. "Torres told me that as he ran from the store the veil that he had worn blew away. When he got to the corner of Seventh and Campbell he tossed the rest of his disguise and the gun in a garbage can." Rosalinda took two slow puffs from her cigarette. "Someone saw him do this, and that person, a man named Obregon, tried to blackmail him. I think that Torres killed him also. I don't know what Torres did with the gold but I think that he did not pay his gambling debt and that is why he was killed."

I listened to Rosalinda's words but I felt no sense of having been proved right. After all, what she was saying was exactly what my own theory had been. Instead, I felt much like a man in some contest who is awarded first place long after the crowd has departed. My dullness of spirit remained. Rosalinda reached over and put out her cigarette in the ashtray. I don't know why, but Rosalinda's lipstick-imprinted cigarette brought to my mind the reason that Penny and I had separated back then. A woman I had questioned in a restaurant had given me a lead on another woman. She had written the name and address of the second woman on a napkin she had used to blot out her bright red lipstick. Penny found this in one of my pockets as she went through them before taking my jacket to the cleaners. Instead of answering Penny's questions honestly and seriously, I had made a joke of it and fueled her jealousy and then one thing lead to another and before I knew it I had packed my suitcase and I was walking out the door. I considered this one of the stupidest things that I had ever done.

Now, Rosalinda looked at Evan. Evan spoke. "Did Tommy tell you how much he owed to the people across the river?"

"Four thousand dollars." Rosalinda did not hesitate.

"Did he, as far as you know, gamble often?"

"Yes, quite a bit."

"I see." Evan paused, and then he moved slightly forward in his chair. "Did Tommy, by any chance, mention to you the significance of the number twenty-three?"

From my position at the side of Evan's desk, I saw Rosalinda's hands flutter but her face was cool as she answered. "No."

"Very well, Miss Lucero. Is there anything else you would like to tell us?"

Rosalinda thought for a moment. "No, Detective Morrow."

"Thank you, Miss Lucero." Evan gave her a smile. "You are free to go then."

Rosalinda hesitated briefly then stood up slowly. She gave Evan a hint of a smile. She did not look at me and then she walked out the door. After two or three seconds, Evan dialed the telephone and spoke into it. "She is leaving my office now." After he put the telephone back on the cradle he spoke to Rudy. "I want you to transcribe Miss Lucero's statement right away. You are to type one copy only and place your notes and the copy into an envelope and seal it and bring it back to me." Rudy looked at Evan as though he wanted to ask a question but then seemed to think better of it and left. I moved to the chair that Rosalinda had vacated. It was still warm.

In a matter-of-fact voice, Evan said. "I have had Miss Lucero under surveillance since she was released from the holding center." Evan smiled at me. "You should feel vindicated, Vinny. It seems to me that what she had to say was exactly what you had suspected." There must have been an unsure look on my face because Evan said, "Is that not right, Vinny?"

"Yes, yes it is Evan. But well, I don't know, something doesn't feel right."

Evan seemed pleased with my words. "How is that, Vinny?"

"Well, for one thing, if Torres was her lover, and the man that she was ready to run away with, why does she call him Torres? You would think that she would call him Tommy or something else. Not by his last name. And, secondly, if Torres was killed over a gambling debt why would they take his notebook?"

"Why indeed." Evan sat silent for a moment. "Miss Lucero has admitted her part in the robbery of her uncle. She stated that her uncle said that the gold would be hers upon his death, and she has the will to prove it. However, in court, her testimony would not be as forthcoming as today, statement or no statement. Besides, I believe her when she says that the person who killed Benavidez did it without her prior knowledge. But, there are two points where I do not believe her, and those are that it was Torres and that she did not know, prior to the robbery, how much was in the trunk. Whoever took the gold had to have had some idea how much was in there."

Evan lit another cigarette. "Miss Lucero has given us a gift in a box with a ribbon tied around it. The problem is that she finds herself in a deadly game not of her making, and that box might explode in her face." With hardly a pause, Evan said, "Vinny, do you know Karen?"

"Karen?" That name was not familiar to me.

"Yes. Tommy's wife."

I had seen Torres' wife at the funeral but I had not approached her to offer my condolences. It had seemed highly hypocritical of me to speak to the wife of the man who I had suspected of murder. I had kept my distance from this black-veiled lady who stood so erect by her husband's grave. "No, I do not know her."

"I was not able to interview her more fully at the time, Vinny. I think that it should be you to go see her."

—— 28 ——

had driven by Torres' house almost every day without knowing that it was his. It was a two-story red brick house that sat back perhaps a hundred feet from Montana Street. I also lived on Montana but further out from town. The driveway up to the house was lined with a short, neatly trimmed hedge, behind which I could see a spacious lawn.

Mrs. Karen Torres answered the door. I had called earlier in the day to make an appointment with her. She was wearing a black dress of mourning. I don't know why, but her appearance thoroughly surprised me. She looked matronly and older than I had assumed. She had a rather plain but kindly face, and she was Anglo. Her eyes looked into mine. The sadness was evident but still she offered me a smile.

"Detective Quiñones, please, come in." She led me into a living room that was furnished with several items of expensive solid oak. She sat in one chair and I sat in another, facing her. Mrs. Torres smiled again. "What can I do for you?"

"Mrs. Torres, first of all, I would like to offer you my sincere condolences for your husband's death."

"Thank you, Detective Quiñones." She paused, "Evan sent you because you did not know Tommy very well?"

"Yes, I think so." Evan had told me that it would be better if someone not so close as himself were to interview Mrs. Torres. I, as a stranger, could ask certain questions of her that Evan could not. That is, I could ask her anything.

I began, as I had rehearsed on the drive over, by telling Mrs. Torres that I had lost my policeman father in a shoot out with bank robbers in San Francisco when I was eleven years old.

"I am so sorry, Detective Quiñones, that must have been very hard." I murmured my thanks. Mrs. Torres removed either a clip or a pin from her hair and let it fall. Our eyes met and I do not know whether it was that gesture or her great sorrow or my deep sense of regret or all of those things combined but at that moment something passed between us; the instant kinship of strangers, a tenderness almost like love.

"Vince?" She spoke my name like a question. May I call you Vince, it said.

"Yes, Karen." I said. We smiled at each other.

"Tommy and I could not have children. I had an accident when I was very young. Tommy knew that and still he married me." From a thick porcelain teapot, Karen poured us each a cup of hot tea. *Would a man married to a woman who could not bear him children become a womanizer?* The thought moved slowly through my mind. I could see where it could.

"How long were you married?"

"Twelve years." Karen took a sip of her tea. "I will not say that we did not fight because we did." Karen smiled. "But the making up was filled with such..." Karen stopped. Then she added, "He had a temper and he was pretty headstrong, you know." Karen looked away from me. A tear rolled down her cheek. I stood up and walked to her and placed my hand on her shoulder. She placed her hand over mine. "I'm okay, Vince." I walked back to my chair.

Karen spoke again. "Tell me, Vince, is it possible for a man to love two women at the same time?" The question startled me. I felt my eyes blink. *What kind of question was that to ask at this time?* I looked at Karen. Her eyes looked into mine, waiting. It took me a while before I finally answered. "Yes, Karen, I think that it is possible."

"Yes?"

"Yes, but for different reasons and differently."

Karen looked into my eyes and held me. "Ah, yes. But one he marries and comes home to, right?" She released her gaze and looked away. "Tommy always came home to me."

I had decided to do my interview as quickly and painlessly as possible but now I perceived that what Karen Torres needed was company more than anything. I relaxed and drank my tea.

Karen spoke softly. "My college friends and I had gone across the bridge to go dancing. Someone tapped me on the shoulder and I turned to look into the most beautiful brown eyes that I had ever seen. He asked me so politely for a dance. Moving around on that dance floor that night I felt as though I was dancing on clouds." Karen paused and looked at me. "I think that most of his life Tommy had this image that he tried to present to others but with me he let me see his heart."

Karen continued to speak of her husband and their lives together. She was right. Torres had presented a side to her that I was sure had not been seen by any other. I let her reminisce for some time and then I nudged her gently toward the reason for my visit. "Karen, I am sorry to have to go into this but yesterday a young lady came into our office and gave us a statement."

"Yes? A statement about Tommy?"

"Yes, we have our doubts about it but as a part of her statement she said that your husband liked to gamble."

A slight frown creased Karen's forehead. It seemed to me that it was not a frown of disapproval but of trying to make sense of my statement. "Gamble?"

"Yes, again, we have our doubts but—"

"Do you mean like a gambler who bets on contests?"

"Yes, like a gambler who bets on horse races and the like."

Karen's hand moved to the side of her face in a gesture of pensiveness. "No, I don't believe so, Vince. I think that I would have known this."

I thought of Pete's words, back on the day that he had given me a ride to the station, that Torres had almost lost his house because of the failure of his private investigator venture and also, according to Pete, through his gambling. It could be a touchy subject for sure. "Karen, please forgive this question, but were you ever in danger of losing your house?"

"This house? How do you mean, losing it?"

"I mean, you know, foreclosure, defaulting on the mortgage."

Karen looked at me, confused. "Vince, we owned our home outright."

I was surprised. "You had no mortgage, no house payment?"

"No. This house was a wedding gift from my parents."

I sat and considered Karen's words. "Karen, when your husband went into the private investigator business, did he maybe put this house up as collateral on a loan, anything like that?"

"No ... I, that is my parents were, well, quite well to do. I inherited money and property from my father. We did not need to get a loan for the business. That money came from my trust."

I went on. "Did your husband lose a lot of money on the business?"

Karen looked at me, the puzzled look returned. "Why, no, I don't think so. I think that he just missed the police department."

"Karen, is it possible that your husband might not have told you everything?"

Karen seemed to have suddenly sensed the exact direction of my questions. There was a controlled anger in her voice. "Whoever has said that Tommy was somehow in debt and needed money is a fool!" I waited a moment or two and sipped my tea. Karen sat up even straighter. The indignation was evident on her face. I was that fool. Why had I not bothered to check on this prior to setting out on my path that led me to Torres? Why? It could have been easy enough to do. I felt the remorse coming again. It seemed to me that Karen's eyes were boring into me. "This is very good tea." I managed to say. The anger left Karen's face and the kindness returned. She smiled at me and refilled my cup.

I had to go on. "Karen, did Tommy ever discuss his cases with you?"

"Once in a while he would. But to be honest with you the act of homicide, the act of one human being taking the life of another, made me sad and uncomfortable."

"Did he mention the latest one? The one he was working on?"

Karen looked at me, seemingly trying to get the words right. "Would it hurt your feelings in any way to consider that Tommy was determined to solve the last two murders on his own so that he could be reassigned as Evan's partner?"

I thought of Torres. I thought of him working his way across the city and across the bridge, asking questions, following leads, pursuing the killer. The prize? Just to get to work with Evan again. The gloom that was always at the back of my mind moved forward. Would that hurt my feelings? No. What did hurt was my own stupidity. I cleared my throat. "Karen, my own feelings are of no importance. All that matters to me is to find whoever did this."

"Yes, Vince. You must find him."

It had been a bright and sunny December afternoon when I had arrived. Now, it seemed that a cloud had covered the sun. The room grew dark. "Karen, by any chance, did Tommy ever leave any of his notes here?"

"Ah, yes. They told me that whoever did this had taken Tommy's notebook." Karen looked at me. Her look had suddenly turned strange. Maybe it was the change in the light. Without a word, she stood up and walked toward a desk and removed a small piece of paper from the center drawer. She walked back and handed it to me and then she sat down on a small couch right next to my chair. The piece of paper was a sheet from one of our standard three-by-five notebooks. It was folded in half. On the sheet was an address, which I recognized as that of Teresa Obregon. It had the date and time. Written below that was my own name and telephone number. Then there was something else written, which had been written with a dull pencil, and which was illegible except for the words "the police". A thought flashed through my mind. I stifled a laugh at the irony of it. *Had there been a time when Torres suspected me?* In a strange way I was hoping that he had because if he had suspected me then we were even. Each of us merely doing our jobs. Yes, Torres and I would be even. Except for one detail. He was dead.

I unfolded the sheet of paper. On the bottom half was the number 23. Karen spoke softly, almost to herself. "Tommy was busy there at the end," she looked away, "he may have gotten two hours of sleep a night, if that."

"Karen, did Tommy tell you who he suspected?"

Karen was not looking at me. She was looking out of the window where there was a rose bush, and where it now seemed that the sun had come back out from behind a cloud. Then it dimmed again and I could see the bush shudder in a gust of wind.

"The wind." Karen said this softly, a faraway look in her eyes. Then she shook herself and came back to me. "That evening he got a call here. It was a young lady. I answered the telephone and handed it to him. Whoever it was I gathered that she had some information for him." I cringed, because that would have been Mona doing what I had asked her to do. "Then Tommy called someone. I don't know who, but it would have to be a police officer because Tommy told him to meet him at the Blue Moon, that he would need help in making an arrest there." Karen leaned back in her chair and closed her eyes. With her eyes still closed she asked, "Do you know who that young lady was, Vince?"

It seemed impossible, and perhaps it was just my overpowering sense of guilt, but at that moment I was sure that Karen knew that it had been me that had gotten Mona to call Torres. I was ready to tell Karen about my involvement in the whole business. I had the urge to unburden myself. I waited for Karen to open her eyes but for some reason she wouldn't. I cannot explain what passed between us there. Me looking at her face, and her sitting there with her eyes closed.

Finally I spoke. "Yes, Karen."

Karen sighed. "Did she have any information?"

"No, Karen."

Karen opened her eyes and looked at me. Her hand trembled as she raised it to smooth her hair back. "Vince, do you know who it was that Tommy called to assist him in the arrest?"

"No, Karen, I do not."

"No, no one knows who that is apparently. Why is that, Vince?"

Two things were obvious to me. One was that it would be in character for Torres to make an arrest in front of a crowd at the Blue Moon. Everyone would know what he had done. May he rest in peace. The other thing was that Torres had thought of the perfect way to get a policeman to a location. Tell him that he needed help in making an arrest. How could that policeman decline? Of the nine individuals left on my mental list I now scratched off four. Torres would not have asked the coroner or the photographer or two others who had left the force to assist in an arrest. That left only five names on my list. The room seemed to move.

"Karen, I would say that whoever it was that Tommy called was the killer." In my mind I could very clearly see the faces of those five men. "Do you remember how Tommy spoke to that individual?"

"What do you mean?"

"Well, did it sound like he was asking or telling?"

"He called from the kitchen. I was in here." Karen paused. "It seemed to me that he had to repeat himself a couple of times."

For a moment, Karen's words floated about the room. I heard them and they meant nothing. Then, slowly, the implication of what she was saying began to insinuate itself into my thoughts. It gave weight to a possibility that had intrigued me as we had gotten deeper into our investigation. I opened my hand and looked once again at Torres' note.

The afternoon moved along. The sun broke through the clouds now and then until the light dimmed and stayed that way. I looked at Karen's face and heard her words but my thoughts were in a different place altogether.

— 29 —

It has taken us three months to finish our work. The holidays came and went. The twelve folders are now in the hands of Evan and Chief Hansen. They are going to study them and then decide how we are to proceed. The strain of the internal investigation had become so intense that the only way to deal with it, apparently, short of violence, was to joke about it. The story making the rounds was that Bellamy had done it. I heard it from Rudy. The funny part about it was how he had done it. Of course, no one ever told the story within earshot of Bellamy. I told Rudy not to repeat the story in front of either Evan or the Chief.

We had completed our files in order of seniority, which meant that Bellamy's file was the first one we had worked on. It had been at that time that a vague but stubborn idea had begun to creep into my thoughts. He, Bellamy, being in charge of the crime lab, knew how the cards had been folded. The starting point all along was that only someone close to the investigations of the Club murders could have known how the playing cards were folded. That premise had been the foremost consideration in the Chief's directive to commence the investigation. We were looking for one of our own.

Jake (his real name was Harlan) Bellamy had entered the force in 1915. In 1924 he had uncovered a small but deeply imbedded pocket of corruption in the police force. There were inexplicable gaps in the file but what I had been able to piece together was that it involved his partner and two others and the chief of police. It had to do with the submission of pay requests. The crooked cops submitted fraudulent requests that were in turn authorized by the chief. Then, the cops would kick back some of the money to the chief. It had been going on for some time and in the end amounted to quite a bit of money. When the smoke finally cleared Bellamy had been given a commendation and a promotion. In Bellamy's file there was an 8 x 10 picture of him standing next to a police car with the framed commendation in his hands. He had been a handsome man.

Personally, after we started into Bellamy's file, I had been of the mind to exclude him because of his age. He had been married to his wife, Gladys, for something like fifty years. Still, as I proceeded with his folder, I discovered that in 1929 one of Bellamy's partners had disappeared without a trace. They, Bellamy and his partner, a man by the name of Rollo Atkins, had agreed to meet across the bridge for a drink after work but Atkins never showed up. Bellamy, being the last person to see Atkins, had undergone quite a bit of questioning back then.

Bellamy's next partner, one Stan Blithe, had accidentally shot Bellamy in the shoulder in a botched up stake out. That partner had retired shortly after the incident and promptly died in a fall from a ladder while working at home. There was another gap and then Evan became Bellamy's partner. I was able to pick up the rest of the story from the archives at the newspaper office. In a strange twist, I discovered that Stan Blithe and the ex-chief, who was then in prison, were married to sisters and those two women were sisters to Rollo Atkins. Penny was fascinated when I told her that story. She thought that there was a whole lot more involved than just fraudulent pay requests.

All of the files had interesting items, some more than others but nothing more. Maybe the Chief and Evan would be able to see something there that escaped me. Maybe, but for me there was nothing that you could hang your hat on. There was just not enough information to point us in any particular direction. I believed we had once again arrived at a dead end.

The three murders in 1950 had occurred within a two-block area on Ochoa Street. The first officers on the scene at each homicide had been partners Teo Steele and Sam Tee. Teo is a big man. He, if he was the one who did Benavidez, would have had to wear a very large dress indeed. Sam Tee might fit the bill. He is the right size and he is thirty-nine years old. According to his financial records he was pretty deep in debt which could be a motivation for robbery. However, it was unlikely that Sam could have left Teo in the car, donned the dress, done the deed, discarded the disguise and so on and so forth without Teo's knowledge. Unless Teo was in on it. That possibility had held some attraction for me, especially when I discovered that Sam, who had lost his parents at a very early age, had been taken in and raised by one of Teo's aunts. I became even more interested when I discovered that Sam had been hired as a cop but quit less than a year later and moved to Los Angeles. I found out that he had worked as an extra in a couple of western movies. He had tried to work his way into being a regular actor but two years later he was back in El Paso and back on the force. Later, I had done an update on Sam's finances and found out that he had whittled down his dept but not by much. So, Sam and Teo remained on my list.

The rest of the files ran about the same way. You could look at them one way and see a glint of something. Then, you looked at them more closely and the light was gone. There was, of course, the possibility that someone who knew how the cards were folded had paid someone else to do it. And, it was also possible that the fifth *Basto* had become involved, as Evan had said on the night we found Obregon. It was an interesting theory but I was not inclined to go in that direction.

Bellamy's file was another matter. It was his file that got me thinking about the possibility that our net had not been cast wide enough. There was something in his file that hinted to me that we had to broaden our search. It was at that time that I had started another folder, one that I kept under lock and key in my desk. I identified it only with the number 23.

In the beginning there were only a few notes in it, shots in the dark. But as time went on it began to grow and become more persuasive. The thing about settling on a particular suspicion is that once you start to focus there you are drawn in that direction to the exclusion of all others. It can be both inviting and dangerous, like when you are walking and finally spot an object of interest off in the distance. You can look away and when you look back your eyes settle on it instantly. It is then when you are liable to step in a hole. So, I had proceeded very carefully with that file. I owed it to Torres to get it right, and beyond that I owed it to Karen.

There were a couple of pieces of information that I needed. One had to do with cards but not playing cards. I knew where to look for that information but I kept putting it off. The second piece of information depended on the first. I think that what held me back was the fact that if I found what I was looking for everything would be clear, and terrible. On the other hand, if the information I sought was exculpatory then I seriously doubted that the murders of Benavidez, Obregon, and Torres would ever be solved.

I took out the folder and looked through it once again. I knew it was time. I placed the folder back inside my desk and locked it. I glanced over at Rudy who was reading something at his desk.

Through the glass partition I saw Evan and the Chief walking away down the hall. I picked up the telephone and dialed the personnel section. I told Mrs. Latham that I needed to look at some time cards. She didn't say yes or no. In a few minutes I made my way downstairs to her office.

The saying that a particular person is not one to suffer fools gladly was invented for Mrs. Latham, I'm sure. Sometimes I wondered if she had been hired after the corruption scandal way back then to guarantee that nothing like that would ever happen again. The personnel section was her domain, period.

Knowing that she would object to my request, I lowered my voice. "Mrs. Latham, this is official business."

"Humph." Mrs. Latham looked up at me over her glasses. She stood up and led me back to a dark corner where there were many rows of black filing cabinets. I was about to tell her that I was only interested in the cards for the fall of 1950 when she opened one particular drawer and pulled it out for me. She stood back but did not leave.

"Mrs. Latham, I am only interested in the cards for the fall of 1950."

"I know."

I smiled at her. "How would you know that, Mrs. Latham?"

"Well, aren't you?"

"Yes. Yes, I am but how would you know that?"

Mrs. Latham looked at me. Her eyes softened just a bit, a hint of pain. "Because those were the cards that Tommy looked at that day."

Torres had not only been a step ahead of me, he had been a mile ahead of me.

— 30 —

Penny and I left the city at five o'clock in the morning. She had wanted us to get away for some time. I felt the same way. I needed speed and the drone of the engine to be alone with my thoughts. I needed to carefully consider what my next step should be. Penny told me she had been interested in the ghost town of Santa Rosa ever since Evan's story about the place. We were to drive out there, spend the day, and then return to the town of Lordsburg, New Mexico where we were to spend the night.

Penny drove, and it seemed to me that I had just gotten used to the highway when we were already in Las Cruces. We went through it before the sun was up and headed west to Deming. The radio was on down low. Over the hum of the engine I heard Penny say, "Get some rest, Vin." I put my head back and closed my eyes. I thought of Torres and how it had seemed to me that I had heard his voice at the wake.

Somehow, Torres had blazed through the process of elimination in a couple of days—a process that had taken the rest of us weeks. Where I had hesitated he had acted quickly. He must have guessed or known that there had to be someone who had seen the folded cards other than the individuals we were interested in. He knew that during the time of the three murders in 1950 the support section of the police department had become overburdened, a matter that the rest of us had overlooked. He must have known that there had been a small number of people detailed on a daily basis from the street to help Bellamy out. And, finally, he knew that the timecards for those individuals for those days would have a different code on them. Whoever he could place in the crime lab at that time would have to be a suspect. Then, it would be a matter of wrapping the circumstances around each individual until he found a fit.

The miles slipped away as I considered each item in my secret folder. I looked at them in every conceivable light. Up, down, forwards and backwards. After a while I blocked them all out and looked at the vast desert plain in the crimson morning light as we drove on.

On the blue horizon directly west of Lordsburg I saw the mountains that Evan's mother had painted. They were unmistakable. We found an old motel with a store and café in the small town and bought some picnic items. We gassed up and at nine in the morning we headed for those mountains.

We crossed the Arizona state line and began to descend slowly down into a green valley with many farms. Now and then I could see the railroad track and thought of Evan. We crossed a bridge over a clear stream and then drove on into a long canyon where we crossed over another stream. The road began to climb again and we went through a tunnel in the side of a mountain. The road took us to an old town with a tilted rotted sign that read Orenville, where there was an abandoned railroad station. We crossed a third stream and then began a winding road up a steep mountain.

I saw a snake sunning itself on a flat rock. Higher up on a rocky outcropping, framed by the bluest sky, I saw a mountain ram. Its curved horns looked golden in the sunlight. A mile or so later, and quite abruptly, we came upon the town of Santa Rosa. Softly, almost in a whisper, Penny said, "This must be main street, Vin."

There were a few concrete and brick structures still standing along a tree-lined street. There were no houses left. Only the rock retaining walls, some with mortar, others without, that rose in levels ever higher above the main street. There were several very steep concrete stairways, cracked and crumbling which seemed to lead up to the sky.

To the left of where we parked there was a small rectangular plaza bordered by large sycamore trees. The air was clean and crisp and smelled of pine. To the right we could see the steep drop of the mountain and then a long canyon with a stream running through it and then a great valley with two other rivers glinting in the sunlight. Very far off the two rivers joined up and then there were more green fields and then there were smooth, golden foothills that looked like folded velvet. Beyond the foothills were mountains with more mountains behind them whose blue almost blended with the blue of the sky. I looked toward the southwest, where I figured the city of Tucson might be. I thought of Evan as a small boy, walking all that way.

"Vin," Penny said breathlessly, "you can see the whole world from here. Smell the air, listen to the quiet." She stretched her arms wide, as though to embrace the panorama. "My God," she said, "I could live here." I did not respond. I was enjoying the feeling of distance and the fact that El Paso felt very far away. Yes, far away. But I noticed that contained in the idea of the city there was also a thought for Rosalinda. I walked back to the car and took out an old army blanket and spread it out over the leaves next to the large trunk of one of the trees in the plaza. I carried the ice chest and placed it to one side.

"Is that a cave over there?" I looked at where Penny was pointing. About a hundred feet away there was a cave with upright rails at its entrance. We walked over. The heavy metal door had been welded shut. I peered into the darkness. I knew that this was the jail that had housed a murderer. A strange old man (a hermaphrodite, Bellamy had said) whose actions had set in motion a long series of events, tumbling down the years to his own death but not ending there. No, it had gone on after that. How many people had to pay for one man's treachery? The air of the cave was cold. For a moment I saw Benavidez' large, round face on the counter of the store that November night. I stepped back. Penny reached for me. "Are you okay, Vin?"

"Yes." I said, and tried to laugh.

We walked back to our picnic area and Penny sat down on the blanket. "This air makes me hungry, Vin. Should I fix lunch?"

"Yes, Penny. I'm going to look around while you do that."

I walked along the main street and at the end the road turned and rose sharply. The road curved back and forth several times and at the top I saw the massive black boulder of which Evan had spoken.

There was a charred and splintered trunk of a tree just before the rock began. The black rock was shiny in the sunlight, as though it was wet. I walked to the edge where the black cliff gave way to a deep canyon. Chiseled into the rock was a narrow path which I followed to a shallow cave. There was a rock- ringed fire pit just inside the cave with ashes and a couple of fire-blackened tin cans. The cave was cool and smelled faintly of decay. I thought there might be a dead animal further back but it was very dark. I did not step in any further.

I came back out of the cave and followed the path that curved around to the other side of the cliff. I stopped almost at the end and peered up over the edge. It was here that Evan had witnessed the horror of seeing his friend killed. And from behind that very tree had appeared the woman in black who had rushed, too late, to Jacob's aid. Very clearly, I felt a young boy's helplessness and terror.

I looked back down the canyon and remembered Evan's words about the wolf and doe, the hawk and the doves. When Evan had spoken about those things, which had been before he told me about Jacob Bingham, I felt that Evan had led a charmed life. I had never heard of nor read of anyone else having witnessed such sights. Later, after he told me the rest of the story, I felt differently.

I came back around and stood on the rock looking down at the plaza. I could see Penny sitting on the blanket leaning up against a tree with her arms propped up back behind her, her face to the sun. I waved but she did not see me. I walked back down the road.

"Is lunch ready?"

Penny spread out our lunch on a linen tablecloth and poured the wine into two coffee cups. She began speaking softly. "Vin. A few minutes ago a small flock of birds just seemed to fall out of the sky. I don't know what kind they are but they've been singing the most beautiful songs. They stopped singing just as you walked up." I looked up into the thick growth of the branches but I could not see any birds.

As we were finishing our simple meal the birds began to sing again. Their notes cascaded down upon us. One particular bird's song caught my attention. His notes were somehow different from the rest. His highs and lows were clearer, purer. I followed his singing and soon the others began to grow faint and then diminished into silence so that only his song remained. I leaned back against the trunk of the tree as Penny placed her hand over mine. The sun was warm on my face. I closed my eyes.

I had never before heard a songbird sing quite that way. It sang a song full of pain and heartache; of good-byes and heartbreak; of hope and falling and failing. It sang of death and losing, and of a morning sun rising. It sang of joy. It sang of finding. It was a rhapsody to things deep within me; things which I had forgotten, or perhaps never knew.

That afternoon when Penny and I came down off of that mountain I had made my decision. We drove to Lordsburg in the dark and checked in at the motel and had supper and went to bed. The next morning we drove back to the city in a dust storm. It was the first day of March.

— 31 —

The next day I drove down to Lola's on Ochoa in search of the answer to my final question. I believed that my theory would hold up even if the answer I was looking for could not be ascertained. It was a minor detail but I did not want it to be a loose end. I parked my car in the small, rut-filled parking lot behind the restaurant, which is a separate structure on the corner of Ochoa and Ninth. It stands apart from the long row of connected tenements. I got out of my car and started to walk. I needed to find out if it was possible to walk from the diner to the location where we had found Obregon by using only alleys. It took a few hit and miss attempts but I finally found the right route and arrived at the narrow alley at the end of which we had found Obregon. A large piece of rusty tin now covered the doorway to the house where Evan and I had interviewed Don Mateo. Walking at a brisker pace, I retraced my steps back to Lola's. I made a note of the time taken and walked into the restaurant.

Lola was sitting at the counter reading the newspaper and smoking a cigarette. Back when Pete and I worked together, we used to frequent the diner at least once a week but I had not been in the place for some time.

"Well, well, look at what some *gato* dragged in."

"Hi, Lola. How've you been?"

"Hey Ida. Get out here and see who in the hell crawled in the door."

Ida came out of the kitchen, took one look at me and said, "No strangers allowed. Don't serve him."

Lola and Ida were sisters and spinsters. They had run that tiny diner since 1938. This I knew because they said it often. They made it sound like it had been fifty years. They joked around a lot, and the coffee and dessert for any cop was free. I discovered that I had missed these two funny women. I had coffee with them and we chatted about things in general. Finally I changed the subject. "Well, ladies, tell me about Pete. Does he still come in here?"

"All the time. Not like some other *sangrones*."

I laughed. "I promise I'll drop by more often."

Ida wiped away at the spotless counter and said, "Drop by or drop away. It don't make me no matter." Then she placed a slice of freshly-baked apple pie in front of me.

A few minutes later I walked out, promising to return soon and bring Penny. Pete's words on the night we had found Obregon, which was November the sixth, played out in my mind. *I'm sitting at my usual diner on Ochoa and I get a call....*

— 32 —

Evan and I sat in the Chief's office and waited as he read my file. I had shown it to Evan first and he had immediately called Chief Hansen and told him we were on the way. What the file showed was that Pete Vereda had been detailed to the crime lab section for two days in November and another day in December of 1950. It also showed that Pete had been off duty (and therefore unaccounted for) at the time of the murders of Benavidez and Torres. The file showed that Pete had been on duty and in the vicinity at the time of the murder of Obregon. Earlier in the day I had gone downstairs and spoken to the coroner. He told me he calculated that Obregon had died at about nine o'clock, maybe a bit later but no earlier. This was interesting to me because Lola's closed nightly at nine. They were pretty punctual about that part of the business. Whoever called Pete on that night would have to see the body, go to the nearest telephone, know that Pete was at the diner, and ask for him specifically. I knew there could be other explanations but they still depended on the fact that the person had to know that Pete was at the diner and the call had to be placed no later than nine o'clock. I had asked Lola and Ida if they remembered the night of November the sixth. Since the murder occurred in the neighborhood, I was hoping that that particular night might still be fresh in their minds. Their answer to me made the question of time irrelevant. They told me they did indeed remember that night very well, and with much sadness. At four o'clock in the afternoon of that day, their father had suddenly taken ill and they had closed the diner and rushed home to be with him. The man died within the hour. The place had been closed from the afternoon of the sixth of November until a week later. Therefore, Pete could not have received a call at that location.

I saw the change in the Chief's face. When he was finished he looked at Evan. His eyes were blinking. "Jesus Christ Almighty, Evan," he said. He looked down at the file again, shook his head, and said, "Will he go down easy or hard?"

Evan lit a cigarette. "I don't think easy, Frank. He's killed three."

"Damn it all to hell, Evan." The chief continued looking at Evan, his front teeth biting down on his lower lip. "We've got to think about this, Evan."

"Yes we do, Frank."

Chief Hansen had been unnerved when he put the file down but now I could see that he was regaining control. He opened a drawer and then closed it. He picked up the folder and looked at it again. I had summarized it down to three pages. On one page was my checklist, the next was a narrative, and on the third page was a timeline corresponding to locations. "Evan. This is strong but circumstantial."

"I agree, Frank."

"What we need, Evan, is for Miss Lucero to name him. That's what we need."

"Yes, Frank. Without that I don't know."

"Do we still have her under surveillance?"

"Yes."

"Who's watching her?"

"It's on a rotational basis. Whoever the shift captain designates."

I had the sense that I knew exactly where the conversation was going and then I had a flashback of the feeling of moving sideways down Stanton on the night we found Torres. I wanted to get up and leave the room.

The conversation went on but neither the chief nor Evan asked for my opinion. I was not asked anything. It was as though I wasn't there. We had coffee and then more coffee. Late in the afternoon the Chief said, "Okay, this is how we're going to do it." He was looking straight at me. When I walked out of the room Evan was on the telephone with Octavio Ochoa.

The next morning the newspapers said that the police department had conducted an exhaustive internal investigation into the death of Detective Torres. The investigation had been started as a result of an anonymous tip. The investigation had been lengthy and expensive but in the end no connection had been found between the death of Torres and the police department. The papers said that at about the same time the police were wrapping up their investigation, a man who was incarcerated in the Juarez jail for homicide said that he had some information about the murder of Torres. The man said that he overheard some men talking and that one of the men said that robbery was the motive and that he had taken Torres' notebook because he thought it was his wallet. The man had then tossed the notebook in the river when he discovered his mistake. The papers said the Juarez police were looking for the man in question. The story went on to say that the internal investigation team had been disbanded and the individuals who comprised the team had returned to their regular duties.

The following Sunday evening I went in to the station for a final meeting with Chief Hansen and Evan. We went through the various steps of the plan. I knew it was too late to back out but the thought still kept jumping around in my head. At nine o'clock I went back to my desk and waited. I couldn't sit still. I walked out of the station and down half a block to a drugstore and bought a pack of cigarettes. The streets were empty. Dusty gusts of wind blew about. A three-legged black cat came trotting by my feet and then went off into a black alley. Walking back toward the station I looked up at the second story and saw only two lights. There is something damned sad-looking about a police station on a Sunday night.

Back at my desk I pulled out my original file and looked at the picture of Bellamy once again. It had been that picture that had started me down the road to my answer. At first, it was simply a matter of being surprised to see Bellamy as a young man. It shouldn't have surprised me but it did. And then, I had the sobering thought that someday I would be as old as he is now. Still, as I had gone back to that picture time and time again I noticed a curious thing. No doubt it was the light or the angle of the picture, but the two-digit number on the side of Bellamy's police car appeared as two question marks. After a while, as I looked at the picture I saw only the question marks. Later, I found out that the "??" was the number 23. That car, the old 23, had been decommissioned at some point in time and replaced with a new car 23. That number plus the fact that Bellamy's file contained a reference to pay cards, as they were called back then, had led me to the answer I looked for and dreaded at the same time.

I sat alone at my desk and watched the second hand move along the clock on the wall. At five minutes after ten I took a few deep breaths and dialed the telephone. My hand was shaking. I heard Rosalinda's husky voice. "Hello?"

"Hello, Rosalinda." There was a pause; I could hear the intake of her breath. She knew who was calling but still she said, "Who is this?"

I spoke very slowly and deliberately. "I need to see you, Rosalinda. It is extremely important." Rosalinda did not speak. I could almost hear her thoughts. "Who is this?" She asked again. I repeated my message exactly as before. Rosalinda exhaled in what sounded like a sigh. "Where?" Her voice quavered and was slightly higher than usual. "I will come out there to you in twenty minutes. You and I are going to take a drive." I paused. "Rosalinda, you must not tell anyone that I am coming to see you." After I hung up the telephone I walked over to Evan's office where he and Rudy were waiting. Rudy looked nervous. I stood at the door. "All set?" Evan asked.

"Yes." I answered. "Are the bridges secure?"

Evan stood up. "Yes." He walked over to me and placed his hand on my shoulder. "Don't take any chances, Vin. You are to call us as soon as she names him."

"Right." I said.

33

The squad car was parked in the shadows of the oleanders across the street and slightly to the north of the store. I pulled up as close as I could to the opening to the back of the tenement. The dispatcher had just finished advising all units that there was a problem with the transmitter and there was to be no further radio traffic until the problem was fixed and he gave the word. I got out and walked toward Pete's car. I held my gun in my hand inside my coat pocket. I tried to smile. Pete rolled down his window.

"Say partner, what brings you out this way?"

Inside of my pockets my hands began to shake but I spoke casually. "Well, I don't know, Pete. I got a call from your subject in there this afternoon."

A small amount of moonlight came through the tall bushes and into the car. I saw Pete sit up. "Yeah? What about?"

"Well, I really don't know partner. Something about something she remembers about the night her uncle got shot. You know how women are. Sometimes they get lonely." Pete looked up at me and cleared his throat but he didn't speak. I went on, "You know how it is."

Pete turned to look at the back of the tenement. My car was blocking his view. His voice was slightly above a whisper. "Remembered something? Like what?" Then he turned back to me.

"I thought we were done with all that shit. I didn't know we were still watching her until Sergeant Gerrard told me to come out here."

"Like I say, Pete, I don't know. But she did say she couldn't talk about it here." I wasn't sure if Pete could see my face clearly but I winked at him and said, "I'm thinking of driving her down to the river." I waited a second, then I said, "Maybe she'll loosen up down there."

Pete made a hissing sound, as though he had started to say something and then cut it short. I didn't wait. I turned to walk away and spoke over my shoulder. "Wish me luck, man." I walked quickly along the path through the oleanders. In the darkness of the bushes, pressed up against the fence, stood a policeman with a rifle clutched tightly to his chest. Neither of us spoke.

I knocked on Rosalinda's door. She already had her coat on. "Rosalinda. You must come with me right now."

"I will not."

"I don't have time to mess around here, Rosalinda." I took her by the hand and led her out.

Then, we were in the car and moving and she was very angry. I think that's what threw me off, her anger.

Rosalinda was wearing perfume, the same one she always wore. I never knew what it was called but it reminded me of roses and San Francisco in the spring. We drove up the street, past the corner of Eighth and Campbell. There was a squad car parked about twenty feet from the intersection just barely within the glow of the streetlight. As we went by the headlights came on and it moved slowly out of the intersection. It turned in the opposite direction and moved down the street away from us and then made a U-turn and began to follow us.

I looked over at Rosalinda, she was looking straight ahead. I began speaking. "How is Benny?" Rosalinda looked at me. Her voice was sharp. "You got me out here in the middle of the night to ask me about Benito?"

I went on. "Rosalinda, I want to help you." She crossed her arms over her chest. "You? Help me? What a joke."

"Believe it or not. I know that you had nothing to do with your uncle's death." Rosalinda made a clicking sound with her mouth. It was meant to convey that my words were of no interest or importance to her whatsoever. I turned right on Seventh and drove past Florence to Ochoa and then made another right and headed back to Campbell. There were police cars in the alleys. I felt better. I felt as though everything was going to be all right.

I spoke again. "Rosalinda, we know that it was not Torres."

Rosalinda looked straight ahead. "I gave you guys my statement."

"Yes, you did. The only thing is that you were not talking about Torres."

Rosalinda looked away, out of the door window. "I'd rather not have to repeat myself."

I drove to the end of Campbell where the asphalt ended and got on a narrow slanting dirt road that crossed the railroad tracks and led down to the river bottom. On each side of the narrow road were tall mesquite trees, thick as a forest. Then there was a large open area where the smooth river rock lay flat and filled in between with sand. The bone-white stones looked blue in the moonlight. My heartbeat began to accelerate.

I drove onto the stones and turned off the engine. The only sound was the sound of the river. I turned toward Rosalinda. "I think we would have believed your story about Torres if whoever killed him had not taken his notebook." Rosalinda continued looking out the passenger side window. She placed her hand on the door handle, as though she was going to get out of the car.

I spoke quickly. "I myself suspected Torres from the beginning. Back when Benny first reacted to the sound of his voice in your room. I did not know then that it had been the *style* of speaking and not necessarily the voice. It is a fact that has caused me a great deal of regret." Rosalinda turned to look at me. I could see her face very clearly in the moonlight. The soft light accentuated her beauty, and it may have only been that light but it seemed to me that her body became less rigid. We sat in silence for a few moments with only the murmur of the river a few feet away. A bittersweet memory came to me upon the sound of the water. Rosalinda and I had come to that very spot one summer night on one of our dates back then. I had the feeling of great distance, as though our date had been a hundred years before. In a different time altogether. The radio was silent. They were waiting for my word.

I took a breath and went on. "Torres was not a gambler nor was he in debt. His wife has money. So, the person who first told me that Torres owed a great deal of money to the people across the river and that he was about to lose his house wanted me to focus on Torres. And then, the second victim, the one who had seen the killer running away from the store had tried to blackmail him. In Obregon's notebook there was only one two-digit number among many three-digit numbers. Then, there was Obregon's statement to his sister. He knew what he was saying. He said that the trail might lead the police to a place they did not want to go." When I said those words I saw a shudder pass through Rosalinda's body.

"Some time back, as I was interviewing Torres' widow, she showed me a slip of paper on which Torres had written the number 23. Then she told me that Torres had called someone to assist him in making an arrest. That would not be unusual but she said that Torres had had to repeat himself. It occurred to me that perhaps the person on the other end could not quite understand why Torres would call him. Who? I thought. Who, among all the police officers would think it strange that Torres would call him? It was at that moment that I knew the significance of the number 23. It was on the side of a police car. Yes, Obregon knew exactly what he was saying when he said the investigation might lead us down a strange path. The Spanish word for path is *vereda*."

I turned once again to Rosalinda. There were tears running down her face, many tears. Then she placed her hands over her face. I reached over and placed my hand on her shoulder. The sobs were deep within her. She opened the car door and sat sideways, away from me. I opened my door and walked around to her side and then I offered my hand to her to help her up. We stood face to face.

"Why?" She said. I knew the question. It was the why of everything. Why did life begin with such promise and end up so badly? Why did we make the choices we made? Why did we meet the person with whom we could spend the rest of our lives too late, or too soon? And finally, why, after we had chosen that person, did they choose another? "Oh Vince, why?" She sobbed and then began striking me on the chest, weakly, each strike a "why?"

My only response was to say her name.

She turned her face away from me. Her voice a whisper. "Do you hate me so?"

I think that I meant to put my arms around her and kiss her on the cheek. But I can't be sure. I really don't know. My mind said one thing and my heart another. Quite suddenly our bodies were pressed together, and then I reached down to kiss her on the cheek and at that moment her mouth met mine and on her lips I tasted the salt of her tears. I was not there. We were not there. We were in a different place.

Rosalinda clung to me as the radio suddenly crackled to life. I was just beginning to turn and go back into the car to make my call when a ghostly figure came walking out from the trees, heading towards the river. He had removed his shirt. It was Pete. The plan had been that when my car passed from the asphalt to the dirt road two squad cars were to seal off Campbell. I don't know how he got through. He was not walking fast but rather in a casual manner. He did not even turn to look at us. I moved Rosalinda to one side and called out, "Hold on there, Pete." He stopped, but without turning toward me he said, "Can't you let me go, partner?"

"No, Pete. I can't do that."

"I saved your life once."

"Yes, you did."

"Not even for that, partner?"

"You know I can't, Pete."

Pete shrugged. In a sad voice he said, *"Orale, esta suave."* Then he turned toward me and I saw the glint of his gun in the blue moonlight. The world stopped, and the hair on the back of my head stood up. A thought jumped into my head, *he's gone crazy!* The world started up again, slowly. Something moved to my right as Pete raised his pistol. His arm seemed to move upward in slow, individual movements until it was level. The barrel of his gun was a large blue circle. *This cannot be happening,* I thought. From another clump of trees a figure emerged. I heard Evan yell at Pete to stop and then I heard Rosalinda scream, "NO!" I reached into my pocket for my gun. I saw the pink flame in Pete's pistol as something heavy hit me in the chest and I began a long, slow fall. My hands were in front of me, reaching for my gun. I could not get it out. I kept falling. I heard another shot and then another. I was still falling. I felt the impact as my head hit the river rock and then the world turned a deep blue and then it exploded into a bright yellow and then blue again and then gray and then the world went black....

When I was able to focus my eyes again I was sitting in the back of an ambulance. The vibration of the siren was drilling a hole into my head. Rosalinda had jumped in front of me and taken Pete's bullet in her side. Evan had shot Pete dead. Rosalinda's eyes were blinking rapidly and there was blood coming from her mouth. My head was pounding. All the food I had ever eaten was working its way up my throat. I kept looking down at Rosalinda as the streetlights flashed by. Her lips moved but I could not hear her words. A Chinese man in a blinding white smock was kneeling by Rosalinda. He had pulled her blouse up and was working furiously to stop the bleeding in her side. All the while the man was yelling at me. "Do not sleep! Do not sleep!" There was a sharp pain in my chest. My eyelids were very heavy. *Was someone crying?* I forced my eyes open but I could no longer focus.

Then I was in a narrow dark place. It was pitch black. A pencil-thin shaft of light began to descend from very far above. It moved jerkily from left to right. Then it receded slowly upward until it disappeared.

— 34 —

I t seems to me that Rosalinda was in a coma for eight days. I've been told that I was out for two. The doctors told me that the bullet had gone in just below her breast on her left side. It had ricocheted off of the backside of a rib and broken up. Part of the bullet, the largest part, had traveled down her side and shattered her pelvic bone. A fragment had exited her body and gone into my chest. The doctor said the fragment in me was small, but that it was imbedded close to the front and side of my heart and that they could not risk removing it.

On the evening of the ninth day, just after I arrived in Rosalinda's room, she opened her eyes. There was a tube in her mouth so that she could not speak. I spoke to her and soon the confused look left her face. Then she began to cry.

In a week or so they removed the tube. In a raspy whisper she asked, "Benito?"

"He is fine, Rosalinda. He is living with Penny and me. We have a spare bedroom."

She closed her eyes. I thought she had fallen asleep. "Will I..." she breathed deeply, "be going to jail?"

She had helped Pete take the gold, which eventually would have been hers anyway, but she had not had anything to do with the death of her uncle. I told her no. I told her that Evan had assured me that he would square everything with the district attorney. Perhaps probation but no jail time. I waited for her to answer but then she did fall asleep.

I seem to remember that Penny began visiting Rosalinda and they became friends. It seems to me that on the day that I introduced them, Penny walked over to the bed and took one of Rosalinda's hands in both of hers and kissed her on the forehead. I remember that Penny would wash Rosalinda's hair and fix it up and apply her makeup. Benny and I would take long drives then or walk about the city or out to the hills.

One day when I was alone with Rosalinda I held her hand and thanked her for saving my life. She said, "If you must know, I tripped into you. I am just so clumsy."

"No, Rosalinda, you are not clumsy. I've seen you dance."

She smiled and then she frowned. "Vincent, I'm sorry about the coffee."

I laughed. "Now that, was clumsy of you." We laughed together and I bent down to kiss her on the cheek. "Now, now." She said.

We were silent for awhile and then she said, "Vincent, can you promise me something?"

"Anything," I said.

"If something happens to me, can you promise that you will look after Benito?"

"Nothing is going to happen to you but nevertheless I promise." There was relief on her face. I went on. "I like Benny very much. I think he is the sharpest little guy I've ever met. Penny just loves him, you know."

"Vincent?"

"Yes?"

"Sometimes at night, when it is very quiet here, I am afraid."

"Don't be afraid, Rosalinda. I am as close as the telephone. You can call me any time. I can be here in five minutes."

Rosalinda smiled and closed her eyes. I looked at her face until she fell asleep.

Rosalinda continued to improve. She had been in the hospital for five weeks when the doctor told me he was confident that she would make a full recovery. I went home happy that night. Penny and Benny and I had a nice supper. After Benny went to bed, Penny and I opened a bottle of wine and took it with us to the bedroom.

The next morning I went by the hospital on my way to work as usual. Rosalinda's nurse stopped me as I walked down the hallway to her room. There were tears in her eyes. She said, "I am so sorry. I tried calling you but the line was busy. Miss Lucero passed away during the night. She just started slipping away. The doctor did all he could. She died at midnight."

I sat on the bench in that long, white hallway. I couldn't breathe. It occurred to me that at the hour of Rosalinda's death, Penny and I had been making love, and that I myself had taken the telephone off the hook.

Evan paid for the casket with the two gold coins. They were worth twenty dollars each. I don't remember the priest's words at the funeral mass or at the cemetery. It was like a dark movie, where everything happens at night. My headache was intense. I do remember that Penny and Benny held each other and cried as the pallbearers lowered the coffin. That, and the sound the chunks of caliche made as the men shoveled the dirt into the grave.

Three days after the funeral, Penny and I submitted our application for Benny's adoption. They said it would take two to three months. In the meantime, they said, Benny would have to stay in a foster home on Dyer Street.

35

I have not been back out on the street since that night at the river. By order of the Chief, I spend my days cleaning up old closed cases and shuffling paper. Rudy comes by for a few minutes every day and we talk but mostly I keep to myself. There are days when I find it extremely difficult to concentrate. Or, maybe it is that I am tired of homicide. The cases are all the same. One man kills another and tries to hide, is found, denies it, and is tried and convicted. Each morning it seems there is a stack of fifteen cases on my desk exactly like that.

I have an appointment once a week with a doctor. I was referred to him by another doctor. Dr. Madrigal takes an x-ray of my chest, from the side, and he says that the bullet fragment it starting to work its way out. He tells me that but he never shows me the x-rays.

He checks the skull fracture on the back of my head. Then he looks into my eyes with a small light and seems to study something in there. He says that the brilliant flashes of white light I sometimes see are a sort of remnant of the swelling of my brain at the time of my fall. He also says that that is what is responsible for my new sense of highly acute hearing. Sometimes I think that the swelling is still there and getting worse because there are some days that I think my head is going to explode. Dr. Madrigal has given me some pain pills for the headaches that follow the flashes of light. I have had to take quite a few. I have not mentioned to him the nightmares. It may be that he has sensed that part of my problem on his own because he says he has a colleague who may be of some help to me. There is no doubt in my mind that he means a psychiatrist.

Sometimes, as I lie awake in the predawn darkness, I can hear the rub of the pedals on the newspaper boy's bicycle from half a block away. In a restaurant filled with chattering people, I can pick out a particular voice and track it and hear every single word as though that stranger is sitting next to me. On the other hand, there are times when I have difficulty in understanding what the person directly in front of me is saying.

I wonder about the blow to my head. I wonder if maybe some kind of connection has been broken. I cannot put my finger on it but it seems to me that a part of me is missing. I look the same, I think, but inside I feel as though I have aged ten years. I cannot describe that feeling but it is a troubling one. I seem to remember a boy in grade school who hit his head on the pole of a swing set in the playground. His name, I think, was Jerry Perry. The kids always picked on him. He was shy and timid, and he was out of school for a week or so. When he came back he was different. He was a different person altogether. After he returned to school I don't think a day went by that he didn't pick a fight.

There are some things that I can only recall after great effort, and sometimes I can only remember things in a roundabout way. I think about Torres and Pete and Rosalinda but it as though I myself did not actually live through those times but rather someone told me about them. They seem as though they happened a very long time ago. Sometimes things flash white and there is no color in the world.

Penny says that I must speak of the dreams. She says that we must try to understand them. But there is no understanding dreams, it seems to me. Somehow, they are yours and not yours at the same time. They have their own reason for existing. My dreams are bizarre. With only a slight variation they are the same, every night.

Still, I try to go on with the business of the day. But there are times when I will suddenly get the urge to get up and walk out of the station. I head toward Stanton, intending to walk all the way to the bridge and back, but I do not get very far. Then I switch over to Ochoa and walk south on it. I am looking for a particular alley. It is a dark alley with a dead end, and on the brick wall at the end there is some writing. I think that maybe there is an answer there. But I really don't know. It is the alley in my dreams. After a while I feel foolish and head back to the station. I tell myself to get hold of my impulses and resolve not to act on them but the next day I am once again heading for Stanton.

I have asked Penny if I make any sound when I am dreaming. She says that I don't, which is very strange to me since it is the effort of my screams that wakes me up. She does say that I sit up very quickly and that is what wakes her. She insists that I tell her the dream. She says that if I speak about the dreams often enough they will go away. I am not sure at all about that.

So, I do not tell her the full dream but just enough so that she will get some kind of idea of what is going on. I tell her that I am on trial and that I have asked the judge why I am on trial and he tells me that I know the reason full well. They wheel in two closed caskets into the courtroom and prop them up against the judge's bench. I demand to know who is in the caskets. And the judge, in a tone that infuriates me, tells me again that I know full well. Then, quite inexplicably, he bangs his gavel and says that I am free to go. Almost instantly, I am in an alley where I have been trapped by a rotund madman who does not walk as men do but rather glides about as though he is on skates. He is my mortal enemy. He moves very quickly. He catches me before I am able to crawl over a high rock wall at the end of the alley. I can hear the crunch of bone when he bites into the heel of my left foot. My cry is the sound of a dog howling. Then, again very quickly, I leave that dream to a place on a great mountain where I stand face to face with a four-foot tall bird that resembles an owl but he is not an owl. He opens one of his wings and there is a kind of writing there, something like hieroglyphics. The symbols are blurry, as though I am looking at them through rippled glass. Suddenly, I realize that it is not glass but water in which I am slowly sinking. The sky through the water begins to darken. It is then that something slimy and cold touches me in the back. I scream in deep water. No, I would rather not tell Penny all of the details.

But Penny was right. The nightmares began to diminish until they went away completely. Then they were replaced by insomnia, which seemed even worse than the nightmares. A hundred thoughts a minute would race through my mind. Images flashed in the darkness. It began to dawn on me that I was going insane.

— 36 —

On the morning after the night Penny told me she was pregnant there was a note on my desk. It said that the Chief wanted to see me. I read the note over and over because it seemed the words moved on the paper.

"Vincent, how are you today?" Chief Hansen stood up and came around his desk to shake my hand. He is a large man, gray-haired, with large hands. It seemed to me that he looked too deeply into my eyes.

"I'm okay." I said, but it did not come out clearly. I cleared my throat and said it again.

"That's good, Vincent. You look good." That cannot be true. I have not had more than one hour's sleep each night in weeks. But then I remember that he always says that. He gestures for me to sit down as he goes back around and sits at his desk.

"Would you like some coffee? How about a drink?"

I said no to each question.

Chief Hansen removed a quart of bourbon from a drawer in his desk and poured each of us drink anyway. He took a sip of his and lit a cigar. I held my drink in my hand.

"Vincent," Chief Hansen said, through a haze of cigar smoke, "sometimes our jobs can get to us."

The thought popped into my head that he was about to fire me. That thought was followed by another: That I didn't care, followed by still another: How would I support Penny and Benny and the baby?

"How do you feel about being a homicide detective, Vincent?"

The question was very baffling to me. I began to ponder it. My mind went in one direction and then another and then another still. After awhile I gave up on it.

The Chief looked at me and waited. My mind started to grapple with the question again.

"I see," he said. "Vincent, have you seen a doctor?"

That question I could answer. "Yes."

"What did he say, Vince?"

"He said that I had a..." I struggled with the word I was looking for. I pondered the word, turning it over in my head, "concussion."

Chief Hansen studied my face. "Vincent, you are a good detective. Evan speaks very highly of you. God knows you demonstrated your capability on the...well, lately." He grimaced. He did not want to say the name. He finished his drink and continued. "I want you to take some time off, Vincent. A couple of weeks at least. Take it easy. Take a trip maybe. A change of scenery. Get this matter behind you. Can you do that for us, Vince?"

A change of scenery. The phrase struck a chord somewhere inside of me. For a moment I was transported back to the mountain town of Santa Rosa. I sat in the sunlight and once again heard that songbird's song. A long, sad note descending.

I came back. My mind seemed to have figured out the Chief's question about being a homicide detective. I began to answer that question. He interrupted me. "I know, I know. But please, Vincent, I want you to take some time off, okay?"

I stood up and we shook hands again. I was suddenly exhausted.

When I got home there was a letter for me from Teresa. It had obviously been written on her behalf by someone and that someone was apparently a calligrapher. In words that flowed like works of art, Teresa told me she had made it to Parral and reopened her mother's bookstore. She said she had heard of my recent troubles and that she had lit a candle at the church for me and that she prayed for my complete recovery. There was an open invitation for Penny and me to visit her. We were welcome at any time.

I showed the letter to Penny. After she read it she said, "Would you like me to respond for you?"

"Yes."

"What should I say?"

"Tell her that time heals all wounds but that time crawls, if it moves at all."

"Vin, I don't think you want me to say that do you?"

An anger I had never known before came over me. I could feel the words forming themselves in my mouth. Ugly, hateful words. I was able to stop them just in time. Or, maybe it was that my throat suddenly swelled up and no words were possible. I saw Penny stand up very quickly and then she was holding me tightly. I wanted to sleep. I wanted to sleep for a very long time.

—— 37 ——

A week after Penny and I were granted Benny's adoption there was a retirement party for Teo Steele. It was to be at the Blue Moon at 2:30 in the afternoon to accommodate all three shifts. Evan insisted that I go with him. I had tried unsuccessfully to find a way not to go, but the day arrived and Evan and I drove down together.

Evan and I sat in his car for a minute or so. The afternoon had grown hot. I could see the heat shimmering off of the sidewalk. Evan spoke. "We've got to do this, Vinny." We got out of the car and walked side by side toward the entrance, past the alley where Torres had been shot. Within those twenty feet of sidewalk I expected the white flash but it did not come. The heat reflection from the sidewalk was intense, and I began to sweat heavily. I thought of Rosalinda, and the way she looked that cold December night when she had waited for me at the bridge. I looked down at the sidewalk, and then Evan and I walked through the swinging double doors together.

Inside, it was cool and dark and noisy. The short, happy blasts of the mariachi trumpets rang out as they began a song. A cheer went up as Evan and I came in and someone slapped a cold beer into my hand. I took a long drink as Mona came gliding by balancing a tray full of empty beer bottles and shot glasses. She winked and smiled and tugged at my tie.

Evan moved off into the noisy crowd. There was loud laughter as Teo stood up and danced with exaggerated movements to the music. I sat at the bar looking out at the party. Rudy came over, beer in hand, an unlit cigar in his mouth. "Damn right, damn right," he said, "I knew you'd make it, Vince."

"What time did this start, Rudy? I thought they said 2:30." I asked.

"Right, but a bunch of us came over at 11:00. We didn't want to be late. You know what I'm saying?" He laughed and then his eyes glistened up. He bear hugged me and said again, "Damn right, damn right."

I sat at the bar and had another beer. Several guys came by and shook my hand and talked briefly. Everyone was in the mood. I could hear laughter come from one table and then another. Everybody had a funny story to tell about someone else.

I walked up the stairs to the second floor bar and ordered a beer. It was quiet and empty except for two young men playing pool. I heard the loud crack at the break and the soft click during play and then the sound the balls made when they dropped into the leather pockets. I drank my beer slowly and watched them finish that game and start another. I was thinking of Penny and Benny. I did not want to think of Rosalinda. I concentrated on the game. One of the boys made a very nice two-bank shot but then missed the eight ball that was pretty much straight away. I wondered if perhaps he was trying to entice the other guy into laying some money down. This got my attention even more.

A voice seemed to worm itself into my thoughts. I turned to one side and there was Bellamy.

"Little birdie tells me you're still having problems with the incident," he said.

He had startled me but I simply said, "Hey, Bellamy. How's it going?"

"You heard me." He said.

I looked at his face. He was well on his way, I thought. His face was shiny and red. His lips were wet with beer.

"How about a beer, Bellamy?" I asked.

He looked away from me and said something that I could not make out. When he turned back to me he had a mean look on his face.

"Don't shut me out, boy."

"Oh, come on Bellamy. We're all here just trying to have a good time." I said. He had made me very uncomfortable all of a sudden. He stood up as though to walk away but then he changed his mind and sat back down on the stool.

"Well, son, I'll tell you how it's going to be," he said. "Either you're going to sit here and talk with me or you and I are going to step outside and you're going to have to whip this old man's ass."

I looked into his eyes. They had turned hard looking. He meant what he was saying. I thought that I would rather shoot myself in the foot than to strike him.

"Damn it, Bellamy, we are talking aren't we?" I said.

He pulled out a pack of cigarettes and offered me one, which I took. He struck a match with his thumb and lit mine and then lit his.

"On this job, sooner or later, you're going to have to go through some shit." Bellamy said this softly, as though he was talking to himself. I didn't say anything.

He took a long drink of beer and spoke again. "What do they pay you for?"

"What? Well, they pay me to be a homicide detective." I said, knowing that our conversation would be over whenever he said it was over.

"And what does a homicide detective do?"

"Jesus Christ, Bellamy—"

"Answer my question."

"Well, shit, investigate homicides." I answered.

"And?"

"And find out who did it and apprehend same." I answered, curtly.

"So, you did what you are paid to do?"

"Well, yes."

"You determined Vereda was involved, you set up a plan, and you caught him, right?"

"Yes." I answered, my voice suddenly husky.

"And he was going to shoot you, right?"

"Dammit, Bellamy, I'd rather not—"

"You would be dead except for the fact that two people saved your life."

"What?"

"The young lady takes a slug for you and redeems herself and Evan shoots a fellow cop before he can get off another shot." Bellamy took a long drag from his cigarette. "Check my math, boy, but I count two people."

I had changed my mind. At that moment there was nothing I would have liked better than to smash my fist into Bellamy's red face.

Bellamy stood up. "What you need to do Detective Quiñones, instead of walking around here like a man who's misplaced his balls, is honor that young lady's memory by doing right by that little boy and run downstairs and fetch Evan a beer and thank him for saving your ass and kiss his hand and try to be of some goddamned use to him, for Christ's sakes."

I stood up. Blood was rushing to my head. "You crazy old sonofabitch!" I said loudly.

Bellamy dropped his cigarette to the floor, stepped on it, and smiled at me. "And with that, Vincent, I bid you a fond adieu." Then he walked away.

I sat back down and looked around. I had cursed Bellamy loudly but the two guys were intent on their game and did not even look my way. The bartender placed a fresh cold beer in front of me without saying a word. I drank it down in two swallows.

I went to the restroom and washed my hands and face. My hands were shaking. I said, out loud, "Crazy old stupid drunken sonofabitch." I washed my hands and face again. I was mad, mad at myself, mad at getting mad. I knew that Bellamy was right, and that was the hell of it. Bellamy was absolutely right.

I walked back out of the restroom and down the stairs. I found Teo, and congratulated him. I began to mingle until I worked my way to Evan. He said. "You about ready to go, Vinny?"

"Yes." I said. "I'd like to stay but I really must be getting home."

"Right, I can take you home and come back. It looks like this could go on for awhile."

— 38 —

The sun had set as we walked across the street to Evan's car. The evening was cool and pleasant and the aroma of baking bread drifted in the air all around us from the bakery up the street.

When we were about two blocks from my house I told Evan to let me out. I wanted to walk the rest of the way. Evan pulled over.

"Evan," I said, "you know, I have never properly thanked you for saving my life." I extended my hand and Evan grasped it firmly and said, "*Orale carnal.*" He said it in a hoarse whisper, in perfect imitation of a pachuco. I smiled.

We were silent for a minute and then I said, "It must have been hard on you, having to shoot him."

"It was, Vinny. But I've come to terms with that. Pete was a good cop gone bad. What can you do?"

"Still…" I didn't finish.

The evening air smelled of spring. The winter had lasted longer than usual. Looking down, I could see the lights of the city beginning to go on. Two cities, two countries, separated by a river. The rest of the gold had never been found. I wondered if it was buried somewhere out there.

"Evan, why did Pete do it?"

Evan looked at me. "For the gold, Vin."

"Yeah, I know for the gold to start with but why did he kill Benavidez?" I was hoping Evan might have the answer to this. I myself could not understand it. I went on. "He had the gold and a plan, Evan. Why not follow that plan and just take the old man back and tie him up?"

"I can't answer that question for you, Vin. But I will say that people, some people, are very complex animals. And a person who steps beyond that line, the moral line that we must all live within, sometimes cannot answer exactly why he did it."

I tried to think of all the time I had spent on and off the job with Pete. There was nothing he had ever said or done that would make me believe he could be a murderer.

Evan began to speak again, and I was reminded again of how much his voice sounded like my father. "Vin, you know that Pete was a crack shot. He was the best shot in the department. He meant, I am sure, to shoot between you and Rosalinda. She moved into the shot. He intended only to draw my fire." Evan looked away, toward the lights of the city. Then he turned back to me. "That is why he had removed his shirt; to make himself more visible in the moonlight. He was still standing after my first shot and could have fired again. He didn't. After my second shot he went down. He was still alive when I went up to him. He did not speak but he offered me his hand. In spite of the two shots his handshake was still strong."

My eyes misted up. I realized then why Pete had raised his gun so slowly. He had been giving Evan a chance to draw his weapon. Evan looked at me and went on. "Rosalinda was an orphan looking for love. Whatever decisions she made, I believe, were driven always in that pursuit. What would we do if we were in her shoes? It was her way out. She told me as much in the hospital. And to her credit she did not try to push off her decisions on to someone else. She took full responsibility for her actions. This may sound strange to you, Vin, but I think that the happiest days of her short life were there in the hospital when you were at her side." I wiped at my eyes with my hand. Evan waited until I got control of myself again. Then he said, "Vin, life can be the hardest damn thing. So hard that it can break your heart. Sometimes things happen over which we have absolutely no control. Do you understand what I am saying here, Vin?"

"Yes, Evan."

"You have lived through a very hard time in your life, Vin. Maybe even harder than I am aware of. A lesser man might not have made it. You are going to be okay, Vinny."

"Yes, Evan. Thank you."

Evan spoke again. "Vinny, you know that I won't be going back out on the street, right?"

"No, I did not know."

"Yes, the Chief has decided that Chief of Detectives is going to be a full time deal. So, what that means is that you are going to need a new partner."

"A new partner?" The thought of another partner other than Evan seemed strange to me.

"Yes," Evan paused, "what do you think of Rudy?"

"Rudy?" I laughed. It had been a long time since I had laughed.

"Yes, the Chief likes him. So do I. He scored high on the test."

"Rudy Tarang?" I asked again. He seemed so young and green to me.

"Yes, Vin. Granted, he's got a lot to learn, but the potential is there. He has the attitude that he can solve any homicide on his own. That is a good trait." Evan waited a second, then he said. "I knew a guy like that, once." Both of us laughed.

We shook hands again and I stepped out of the car. I began walking toward the house. There were young girls, in twos and threes, out walking along the street. Boys on bicycles whizzed by them, zigzagging, some standing on their bicycle seats, going fast, showing off.

I could see the light in the kitchen. I thought of Penny putting supper on the table, moving slower now, beginning to show. Penny said she knew it was a girl, and, she said, the midwife down the street agreed. Penny had picked out a name. Our daughter's name would be Evangeline Rose.

Benny was waiting for me on the porch and ran out to meet me. We shook hands and he placed my hand on his shoulder as though to assist me in walking.

"How was your day?" Benny asked.

I smiled. "Good. All in all I had a good day, son. And yours?"

"Good also, thank you. Very good."

"Is supper ready?"

"Yes. Mom made a roast and mashed potatoes and a cherry pie."

"Good deal. I'm hungry, how about you?"

"Me too. I am hungry too..." Benny paused a moment then added, "Dad."

At supper, Penny was being very witty. She made Benny and I laugh. Her apron accentuated the swell of her belly. She had a glow to her that filled the room.

Later that night, in bed, as Penny and I held hands in the darkness, I heard the rising and swirling and falling of the Santa Rosa bird's mystical serenade. It was like a distant echo inside my head. It grew fainter and fainter until it was replaced by the sound of a siren, faraway downtown. For the first time in months I felt the hint of anticipation at that sound. I thought about Rudy and laughed.

"What's so funny?" Penny squeezed my hand.

"Oh, I was just thinking about Rudy."

"Rudy? What about him?"

"Well, I think that he is going to be my new partner."

Penny laughed. "Really now." She seemed to think about it for a second. Then she said, "Well, I guess all I can say is that those blankety-blank criminals better keep their blankety-blank ears covered."

"Blankety-blank, Penny?"

"That's what I said."

The night grew very still again as Penny turned her body towards mine. I could smell the fragrance of her hair. A soft breeze came in through the open window, carrying with it the smell of honeysuckle and roses. There was a fullness to the night and the bed and Penny. I reached for her and touched the firm roundness of her belly. She pressed closer, tight against me. I felt her heartbeat. Then everything else slipped away and all I knew was rhythm. All that remained was the steady rhythm of Penny's heart.